REMBRANDT'S MODEL

Rembrandt's Model

A NOVEL

Yeshim Ternar

Véhicule Press

The title page drawing, "The Jews in the Synagogue"
is by Rembrandt van Rijn.
"3 Poems of Sabbatai Zevi" from *Exiled in the World*
© 1989 by Jerome Rothenberg and Harris Lenowitz, eds.
Excerpt reprinted by permission of Copper Canyon Press.

Véhicule Press gratefully acknowledges the support of
The Canada Council for the Arts for its publishing program.

Cover art direction and design: J.W. Stewart
Cover photograph: Thomas Königstahl, Jr.
Photo of author on page 175: Roy Hartling
Cover imaging: André Jacob
Typesetting: Simon Garamond
Printing: AGMV/Marquis Inc.

CANADIAN CATALOGUING IN PUBLICATION DATA

Ternar, Yeshim, 1956-
Rembrandt's model
ISBN 1-55065-101-3

I. Title

PS8589.E745R45 1998   C813 .54   C98-900194-6

Published by Véhicule Press
P.O.B. 125, Place du Parc Station, Montreal H2W 2M9
http://www.cam.org/~vpress

Distributed in Canada by General Distribution Services
and the U.S. by the LPC Group

Printed in Canada on alkaline paper.

Contents

Acknowledgements

Many friends and many kindred spirits both from the present and the distant past have supported this book. I would like to thank Aron Rodrigue, Noel Delcourt, Rose Marie Stano, Cumhur Oner, and Semiramis Muhurdaroglu. Joan McSheffrey, who was my first reader, gave me unwavering support throughout the writing. I am grateful to her for her many valuable suggestions.

I would like to thank my publisher, Simon Dardick and Vicki Marcok, my editor and friend, for their dedication and support.

I felt the presence of Sealiah, the guardian angel of my hero, hovering over me with love and humour as I wrote this book. I acknowledge also the spirits of Rembrandt, Sabbatai Sevi, Menasseh ben Israel, and Charles Maturin.

Sections of this book are based on historical research which I wove into the fiction. I thank especially the following scholars: Simon Schama, Gershom Scholem, Yosef Kaplan, Cecil Roth, and Anthony Bailey.

Finally, I thank The Canada Council for the Arts and the Conseil des arts et des lettres du Québec for financial assistance.

ONE

Chalcedon

SARA SAT ON THE BED in the guest room of her friends' house in Bebek, close to the Bosphorus University, and unfolded the map of Istanbul. During her first week she had already done four of the day trips recommended by the Knopf Guide. She had seen the Haghia Sophia and the Topkapi Palace in one day; the Blue Mosque, the Basilica Cistern, and the Grand Bazaar during the course of another. Then, on a sunny, crisp Friday morning, she had decided to stay close to home and trekked to the Rumeli Hisari, the Fortress of Europe which was built by Sultan Mehmed II, the Turkish conqueror of Istanbul.

The fortress had been nearly deserted, with only the guards at the gate. An elderly British couple had briskly climbed up the citadel's steps ahead of Sara, undaunted by the sharp October wind blowing from the Black Sea. Afterwards, on the way back, Sara had spent a good part of the afternoon sipping tea in a tea house snugly nestled midway up the side of a hill with an excellent view of the Bosphorus. There she had again found herself alone, in part because she had chosen to sit outside. With her jacket zipped up and her face to the sun, it had been pleasant to watch the slow traffic of tankers, passenger ferries, and fishing boats up and down the Bosphorus, a welcome contrast to the bustle of tourists and hawkers who she had encountered in her forays to the usual tourist sites.

Sara had taken a year off to travel before starting her Ph.D. Istanbul was the last leg of her trip. She was fascinated by everything about the city, particularly the fact that it embraced two continents, Asia and Europe, and had ruled large regions of both when it was the capital of several long-lasting empires.

Sara's guidebook had a section on Istanbul as seen by writers and she made a reading list. She noted two excerpts from two novels by Pierre Loti, the turn-of-the-century French writer who had loved this city and its inhabitants. On her fourth day of excursions Sara had gone to the famed Pierre Loti Café after exploring the recommended sites along the Golden Horn where the Bosphorus arches like a crescent to form the ancient harbour of Istanbul.

Where should she go next? She could go to Galata, Pera and Taksim, but these were congested business districts and Sara wondered if she was up to it. She glanced at the map to where she had been that day along the Golden Horn. Oddly, the guide book only mentioned the sites along the southern bank of the Golden Horn, which she had visited all the way up to Eyup and the Pierre Loti Café. What was along the northern bank? The area on the map depicted a huge green space filled with L-shaped symbols which caught her eye.

According to the legend at the top left corner of the map, the symbol designated Jewish cemeteries. The cross was used, obviously, for the Christian cemeteries, and the angular U shape for the Muslim cemeteries. It was hard to tell the Muslim and Jewish cemeteries apart at first glance. The Jewish cemetery was situated directly across from the holy Eyup cemetery on the northern bank of the Golden Horn.

Sara searched for a reference to the Jewish cemetery in her guidebook; there was none. She was surprised that such a large plot in this congested city had been apportioned to a Jewish burial ground. If it was across from the Eyup cemetery, she assumed, it must be just as old. At one time there must have been many Jews in the city. Perhaps a large community still existed. She decided to go to the Jewish cemetery the following day. Why not? It would be something different, it was unlikely to be very crowded, at least by the living.

Sara folded the map so that the section with the cemetery and the Golden Horn faced up. She placed the map and her guidebook on the bedside table, turned off her reading lamp, and slept.

In the middle of a moonless night in October, Sara opened her eyes in the Jewish cemetery on the northern hills of the Golden Horn. She had been lying on a horizontal slab of marble, a gravestone inscribed with the story of the dead woman who lay underneath, as is the custom of Jews in that part of the world. The woman who lay in the grave had loved the roses and other precious flowers in her garden but the tulip had been her passion. She had loved her husband dearly although he had abandoned her to accompany the messiah to Albania; she had loved the messiah who had separated her husband from her. The messiah had warmed her heart more than her own sons although they were honest men and well-known in Constantinople, one being a musician on the kitara, and the other, a scribe. "Oh, loved one, (mi querido)" ended her story, "keep me in your embrace, forever."

The woman had died recently. Rain and wind had not yet

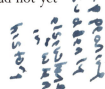

softened the edges of the newly-carved letters on the grave stone, so a gentle wandering of fingers over the letters would have conveyed their message, even in the dark. As Sara's bare back was directly in contact with the letters, she had absorbed the story through her skin. When she came to and rose on her elbows to observe her new surroundings she was imbued with a passion for tulips and a keen love for the messiah.

An ancient woolen cloak embroidered with the many names of God in golden thread covered Sara's nakedness like a blanket. Her golden hair, falling like a cascade over her face, had shielded her features from the spiky chill of starlight as she slept. Sara's bare feet protruded from the hem of the cloak, sore and bruised from the rocks and weeds that had scraped her flesh during her journey across the mountains. Although she had been transported by gales across the Balkans, she had touched down on earth for an occasional respite and a meal which had been miraculously delivered to her by an old male stork who bore a striking resemblance to her long dead father, God bless his soul. Sara sat up on the slab of marble and slipped the cloak over her head. She cinched it at the waist with a silver buckled belt that was already looped through the middle of the garment. She had no reason to be ashamed now, if human eyes spied on her in the middle of the cemetery.

Tumbleweeds rolled in the wind. "Sara, Sara," whispered the wind as it rustled the short stalks of dry thistle grass grazed to the ground by the cemetery guard's goats. In the darkness Sara heard the rhythmic sound of footsteps crunching the dry earth. It is probably my father, thought Sara, for her father appeared to her every time he considered it necessary to guide her, although he had been dead for many years.

He had appeared to her when she was in Amsterdam, a fourteen-year-old girl engaged to be married to the son of the

Polish woman who had raised her as a Christian after she was orphaned at the age of eight. He had advised her to break off her engagement and go east where she would find the king of Jews, the long-awaited messiah, and marry him, for she was destined to be the queen of Jews. As soon as she had agreed to follow his advice, a strong wind had swept her up, billowing her skirt around her thin legs. In an instant, she was hovering above the thin spires of the Protestant churches, and the leaden canals below her looked as if they had been etched into the earth with a blunt-edged burin. She was scared and cold from the winds blowing in from the open sea. She begged the invisible force that was transporting her to bring her down and was promptly deposited in Livorno where she stayed for the next two years working in an almshouse run by elderly nuns.

When evil tongues started wagging, accusing her of having bedded with the beggars she fed, she asked to be delivered to her groom, for she was ready and no longer frightened. As soon as she wished this, one night as she stood alone in the plaza at the centre of Livorno, she was lifted once again. The lazy pigeons who roost in the plaza awakened to the turbulence of her departure and took flight in the whirlwind that thrust her upwards.

The pigeons of Livorno had witnessed what happened to Sara that night, but they could not dispel the curiosity of the gossip mongers in town, for the language of pigeons is unknowable to humans who use their tongues to peck at other people's honour.

"Harlot, harlot, she was a harlot," wagged the tongues in Spanish and Italian, and Hebrew, and all the other languages the Levantine Jews use among themselves, as Sara flew across the Balkans toward Constantinople. Sara disregarded them although at times they howled louder than the gale that was carrying her to her destination. She was immune to their condescension. She would be the queen of Jews as her father, God bless his soul, had told her.

The footsteps came closer. Sara expected to see her father, coming to give her a fresh set of instructions. She was startled by the touch of a wet nose on the soles of her feet, then a tongue, enthusiastically licking. She peered into the darkness at the edge of the marble slab and came face to face with a goat. She assumed it was one of the goats kept by the cemetery guard. Being shorter than the marble sarcophagi that stretched as far as the eye could see, it had traveled undetected on a labyrinthine path only a goat could master.

"Sara," said the goat, for the goat indeed looked and sounded like her father, "go back to sleep now. The nights in this city are longer than the nights you have known. When you wake at dawn, stretch your muscles well, for they will be sore. Go to my master. Although it will not be the same man who is on duty in the morning, it will be a goatherd who keeps a flock of goats in this cemetery. He is to be trusted. You will meet your king. He will recognize your signs and speak to you."

When she met Ali, Sara was standing at the gate at the south wall of the cemetery gazing at the calm waters of the Golden Horn shimmering in the noon light. Ali sat by himself inside the gate on a block of marble, watching the group of tourists he had brought to the cemetery wander about in the narrow passages between the graves. They stopped here and there to snap the occasional photograph of a long epitaph in Ladino. He noticed an overweight woman away from the others furtively rubbing charcoal on a piece of white canvas she had placed over the headstone. He had expressly requested that they refrain from doing this. On the way to the cemetery, he had stood at the front of the tour bus as usual and explained that rubbings eroded historical monuments, and that as a courtesy to the following generations of tourists, they should avoid destroying historical artifacts. A small group gathered around the offender who quickly folded her sheet of canvas and stuffed it into the pocket of her windbreaker. He decided not to confront her.

Sara watched Ali observing the tourists. She liked the way he scratched his head as he thought about what to do with his wayward flock. She liked his long fingers and the silver ring on the middle finger of his right hand which accentuated the gentle flow of his hands. The ring had a large letter "A" carved into its centre. She decided to ask him what it signified.

"I inherited this ring from an ancestor who had the same name as I," he replied in perfect English, his handsome angular face glowing in the sunlight when he turned toward her.

"Which is?"

"Ali? And yours?"

"Sara."

They started talking. Ali asked her all the usual questions: where she was from, where she had been, how long she was staying in town. She told him of her travels and the friends she was staying with in Istanbul who taught at the Bosphorus University. He invited her to join his group of tourists for the afternoon and then have dinner with him at the end of the tour. Sara trusted him intuitively. Although he talked with ease and confidence, Sarah detected an underlying shyness, perhaps even insecurity. She felt that he would not knowingly harm her. She accepted his invitation.

They met again a few days later in Sultanahmet at the Pudding Shop. As they drank tea at a table by the street, Ali said he wanted to take her home. Sara said she would feel uncomfortable meeting his family so soon.

"You're not going to meet my family," Ali answered.

Sara was puzzled. "Where are we going, then?"

"Home. The house where I grew up. I want you to see it."

"Won't there be anyone there, at all?" she asked, hesitantly.

"No," he answered, amused that Sara had assumed she would meet his family. "They have all moved to the city for the winter. By the first week of October, they all move out of the house. I'm the only one who lives there during the winter."

"The only one?"

"Yes. I am the only one who likes to be alone in that house. It's huge and quite old, and very drafty during the winter. It doesn't have central heating, so the kitchen is the only place where it gets warm enough. I sleep there during the winter, behind the stove."

Like a cat, Sara thought. "Are you the caretaker?" she asked.

"You could call it that," he answered. "I like the house. I like the quiet, and I am not scared."

"What's there to be scared of?" she asked.

"Like I told you, it's quite big. As you have probably figured out by now, Turks don't like to be left alone. They consider it a punishment." He chuckled. "And then, the house is special. You see, it's been in my family for 300 years or so, and sometimes its history is too much to bear, especially if you're alone in the house and you hear nothing but your own breathing and the wind rattling the windows."

"But you don't mind?"

"No, I don't mind," Ali smiled mysteriously. "You'll enjoy the ferry ride," he added. "That's why I told you to bring along your windbreaker. If it stays sunny like this, it'll be pleasant to sit on a bench on the deck. That's my favorite spot on a ferry."

16

"I took a ferry the other day," Sara confessed, "when you were busy with the group of German tourists."

Ali was puzzled. "I thought you said you were going to spend the afternoon at Beyazit library?"

"I changed my mind. It was too beautiful to spend the day indoors. I can't read most of those books, anyway."

"I hope you won't be bored in Buyukada, then."

"Buyukada?"

"Prinkipo, the island, the largest of the Prince's Islands."

"I'm looking forward to it! My guidebook says it's one of the few places left around Istanbul untouched by urban development."

"But I'm taking you there to show my library."

"That's fine, too," Sara said, and leaned across the table and kissed him congenially on the cheek. She trusted him because of the dream. She always trusted her dreams to protect her even among strangers in a foreign country.

When the ferry docked at Buyukada a dour attendant in a steel blue uniform opened the wrought-iron gate of the port to allow them passage onto the island. They walked a few paces under the open sky before entering a sparsely decorated terminal building which most likely was built at the turn of the century by a progressive public works department staffed by Ottomans eager to catch up with the West.

The other passengers who had disembarked at the same time rushed through this terminal which was more a hallway than a waiting room. Sara dawdled, staring at the large vein-like cracks on the ceiling which had been patched in places by a lighter shade of plaster, the dull light-beige faience tiles on the walls, and the light fixtures that were part chandelier part street lamp. She was fascinated by a large woman who sat alone, reading a newspaper by the light of a dim bulb, in a cramped stall lodged in a cubby hole in the wall. In the display case under the wooden counter on which she rested her bare arms was a bewildering assortment of items: chewing gum, aspirin, socks, condoms, sewing supplies, Coca-Cola, and comic books.

When Sara looked behind her she noticed the same solemn attendant closing the island gates. He slipped a chain through the baroque curlicues at the centre of the filigreed gate and fastened its last two links with a padlock. With this, Sara felt locked into a peculiar dimension of reality that calmly, methodically, regulated intrusions from the outside world.

Ali led Sara up a winding street lined with old wooden houses whose sagging balconies formed an awning over them. The street was paved with cobble-stones, and although time had worn them smooth and flat, they were not even. Sara was compelled to keep her eye on the ground to avoid twisting her ankle. There weren't too many people on the street despite the fact that it was a pleasant October day. Sara thought it odd that such a beautiful place was abandoned simply because another season had arrived. Perhaps Ali was right, the pull of Istanbul was too hard to resist once winter came. Remaining behind would mean embracing loneliness, a state unbearable for a people who all seemed to have a decidedly melancholic bent.

Up the hill the houses were further apart and no longer uniform in style. Some were closer to the street, some deeply recessed behind sizeable front yards sheltered by trees and bushes. Ali told Sara that in the spring, when the flowers bloomed and the fruit trees blossomed, these houses were barely noticeable behind the profusion of colour. He explained that the original owners centuries ago had preferred to conceal their property behind the wealth of nature, not because they wanted to disguise their lives behind the trees, but because they believed that nature in its abundance was more worthy of display than anything human hands could build.

Ali held Sara's hand tightly. Sara wasn't used to holding a man's hand like this. None of her previous boyfriends had been comfortable with demonstrations of affection in public because it wasn't politically correct in her circle of friends. Such a simple thing as holding a man's hand had become fraught with ideological garbage. But she felt that in Istanbul, because she was a tourist, she could defy all her previous conventions.

A strong wind blew from the sea. Ali checked to see if Sara's windbreaker was zipped up. "You have to be careful about the wind on this island," he said. "It's always cooler here than the mainland. I don't want you to catch a cold."

Sara's hand sweated in his grasp. How far could this hill continue, she wondered. From the ferry, it had appeared steep, but the distance had deceived her and she had assumed it would be much easier to climb. Although they had paused several times to catch their breath during their ascent, Sara needed a longer break. But Ali urged her on. He pointed to a grove of chestnut trees to their right, through which a barely visible path lead down the hill. "Over there," he said. "You can't see it from here, but it's right below those trees."

Sara doubted him. She trusted him to take her to the house eventually, but she doubted that it was as close as he claimed. When they reached the grove of chestnut trees she still hadn't seen any sign of a building. They walked a few paces down the path, turned to the right, and then, just as Ali had promised, there it was: a magnificent old house built on the side of the hill.

It reminded Sara of a ship, an ark perhaps, and she wondered why. Then she thought of the old ferries plying the Bosphorus, criss-crossing the narrow strait. She had observed them emerging from the blue, looming, bent on a crash course, headed to shore. In the week since she arrived in Istanbul, she had stood several times on a ferry landing, wondering if she would be hit by a ferry and die like that, in a naval accident, without even leaving land. But before she was able to imagine the sensational headline such an accident would create, the ferry was always manoeuvered away. When it stopped, engine idling, hull secured to the shore by hawsers flung around massive bollards, and wooden ramps pushed on its deck from the shore, the ferry had already turned its nose at the other shore. Her legs swayed from her imagined ordeal, she tried to maintain her balance on the ramp as she walked in the midst of the crowd pouring onto the ferry.

Further down the hill the gentle slope ended abruptly at the edge of a sheer cliff. If the end of the world could be imagined as the sharp cut-off point beyond which human life was not possible, it was to be found here at the side of this hill in Buyukada where this old house stood as the last outpost. But the faint skyline of the ancient city on the horizon challenged the possibility that one was completely alone in the world.

Ali led her up a stairway at the side of the house. He said he preferred using these stairs, although they were narrow and worn out, to the more formal stone steps at the front of the house. Going up the steps behind Ali, with the sea behind her shoulder, Sara felt as if she were climbing the gangway of a ship. At the top of the stairs Ali dug into his pants pocket and produced a bunch of keys. He separated two that were unusually long. The keys looked unlike any Sara had seen before in Istanbul. They had exceptionally long and slim stems as if they were meant to open locks set in the depths of massive doors. Ali chose the longest key to open the first door. Once inside they were in a small vestibule barely large enough for the two of them. A second door faced them. As Ali fumbled with the lock Sara examined a delicate design inlaid with cherry wood on the door. Although it looked like an abstract geometrical design at first glance, she guessed that it was a segment of stylized script. She asked Ali if the marquetry signified anything.

"My name," he answered, matter-of-factly.

"How could this be your name? It looks at least a century old, if not more."

"It is," Ali chuckled. "In fact, It's much more than a century old. It's over three hundred years old."

"Your name?"

"Ten generations old, my name. This house belonged to an ancestor of mine who came to Istanbul from Spain."

"You're Spanish?"

"Of course I'm not," Ali said. "I'm as Turkish as they come. The man who put his name on this door was also Turkish, a faithful servant of the Ottoman Sultan Mehmet IV, otherwise known as Hunter Mehmet."

"Was your namesake a hunter as well?"

"Not at all," Ali answered. "My namesake was a customs broker at the port headquarters, close to where I met you today."

"And he came from Spain?"

"That's what we believe."

"And he was a Muslim?"

Ali smiled. "I'll tell you all about it, " he said, "but first, I want to show you my house." He opened the door. It led directly into an old kitchen which still retained its original trough-shaped enamel sinks, racks on the walls where plates stood upright side by side, and huge hooks from which hung ladles and pots. A round stove at the centre of the kitchen, polished black by years of use, served as a hearth as well as a cooking stove. A thick flue pipe rose from its back. Approximately a foot below the ceiling, it joined an equally large horizontal pipe through a massive elbow fitting. The horizontal pipe crossed the remaining length of the ceiling before disappearing into a hole in the wall ringed by concentric circles of soot.

"I have never seen anything like this," Sara said, in awe.

"I don't think you could have," said Ali. "Very few houses in this city have their original fixtures."

Behind the stove Sara saw a double mattress on a simple steel frame. "Is this where you sleep?" she asked.

"Yes," he said, "I've spent the best part of my life here."

"Sleeping?"

"Reading. That's part of the deal. Whoever agrees to take care of the house must continue reading the books."

There were no books in sight. The kitchen offered no hint that it was a place for reading. Although Sara saw neither magazines nor newspapers, she conceded that there was a peculiar serenity in the air which is more appropriate to libraries than kitchens.

"Come I'll show you the rest," Ali said. "Although I wanted to offer you tea first, I think you're ready to see the library." He dug into his coat pocket and produced the same bunch of oddly shaped keys which he had used to enter the house. This time he picked a shorter, flat key and opened the door at the other end of the kitchen. Then he unlatched a heavily padded second door which opened into the adjoining room. "We have to safeguard against fire," he explained. "This way, the library is virtually fire-proof."

The only piece of furniture Sara could see through the door was a grass-green armchair upholstered in the same coloured material as the wall-to wall carpet on the floor. The chair faced the large windows overlooking the Marmara sea. Although the winged armchair was the only piece of furniture at the centre of the room, it wasn't the most unusual thing about the room.

Behind the armchair, along the wall, there were wooden cabinets stacked with books from floor to ceiling. Some were thick tomes, bound in leather; some, folios tied with strings; and others, loose leaf manuscripts kept in folders made from marbled paper in iridescent hues.

Each section of books was described by an unusual heading. One sign announced in French, "Rêves" ("Dreams"). Another, "Il faut vivre avec ses amis", ("One should cultivate friendships in life"). There were signs in English: "Metaphysics" and "Geography"; and in French once more, "Vin du Pays"!

Who had collected such books? The pretense of importance angered Sara. What had Ali taken her for? A fool who was ready to admire everything in a foreign country just because it was different? How could anyone consign his lifetime to reading the dated volumes from this odd, eclectic library? At best, these books could provide amusing summer reading, not a lifetime of serious study.

Sara approached the section closest to her—"Dreams." Ali didn't say a word when she reached over and scratched her fingernails on the wooden surface of the book. Horrified, she saw that she had scraped tiny flakes of gold paint from the spine of the book she had hoped to retrieve.

She heard Ali laugh behind her. "The real books are inside," he said.

"What do you mean?" Sara's voice rang with frustration.

"You have only scratched the surface of the library!"

Ali reached over and applied pressure with both thumbs to the top of the shelf under the sign of "Dreams." A door sprang open. Behind the illusory bookshelf was another bookshelf containing books that were less neatly stacked. He pulled out the first volume, an old book with wavy, yellowed pages whose edges were unevenly cut. He opened the book to the title page and showed it to Sara. It read, in woodblock lettering, "Piedra Gloriosa O, de la Estatua de Nebuchadnesar." The date underneath was 1655; the author, Menasseh ben Israel.

"This is one of the first books acquired by this library," Ali said.

"When?"

"Around 1680 or so when a man named Salih Effendi bequeathed this book and many others to my namesake Ali Effendi. They were best friends when they were in Spain, and later, they met again here in Istanbul."

Sara opened the book which Ali had put in her hands. Placed in the book were four engravings depicting winged creatures, ladders, lions, a warrior, and a statue; all signed by Rembrandt Van Rijn.

"Are these real Rembrandts?" she asked, astounded.

"They certainly are," said Ali. "We believe that Salih Effendi knew Rembrandt when he was in Holland."

Sara found it hard to believe him. How could anyone claim a family link to Rembrandt so casually? Especially in a city so far from where the great master had lived and painted. If what Ali was saying was true this book was priceless. And yet it was kept in an old house, in a strange wooden cabinet behind an incongruous epithet, where very few people knew it existed.

Ali gently patted her head. "Sara," he said softly, as if he were trying to calm a child. He took the book from her hands and led her to the green-winged armchair at the centre of the room. Gently pressing on her shoulders, he made her sit down. When she settled in the chair he handed her the book. "Here," he said, "take it and savour it."

From where Sara sat she saw the blue-green sea stretch out ahead of her, free of boats and ferries. Whitecaps danced on the horizon under feathery clouds sprinting across the sky. She settled in the chair which firmly supported her back. She deliberately pressed her feet on the carpet. She was confused because she felt it was as if her feet had sunk among tall stalks of grass. She knew this was an illusion, but she didn't care.

Ali was so quiet that she couldn't even hear him breathe. The only sound in the room was the crackle of the pages as she turned them. After she was through with the book containing the Rembrandt etchings Ali handed her another book, a dog-eared copy of Aesop's fables in Latin, published in 1621.

Hours passed as Sara browsed through the books in the library. Within their pages she smelled the dust of the journey that had brought them from the cities in the West where they were published to this island where Europe ended. She traveled to the point in time when these books were but seeds in the imaginations of their authors. She sensed in her own muscles the tenacity with which a writer shapes with his sentences the languages available. Within her forehead she felt the force of the will which sustains a book as it is being written, and in her heart the energy which hurls it across centuries.

Ali brought her one book after another from the shelves behind the cabinet doors whose trompe l'oeil facade had fooled her completely. Without the illusory library, these mysterious books would not have survived through the centuries. She imagined with delight the curiosity seekers and suspicious government inspectors who would have been foiled by the harmless titles they saw when they stuck their heads into the room.

Ali waited on her like a messenger determined to deliver an important missive. He was patient when Sara lingered over the pages of a book whose illustrations held her attention more than the others. He did not insist that she examine one she had laid aside because its brittle spine had made her nervous. Several narratives caught Sara's attention and, although they were in

Spanish, she tried to read them using her boarding school French. She realized halfway through that the original stories must have been conceived in Hebrew before they were translated. An author by the name of Luria had composed a rainbow calendar, whose months Sara ascertained through the emotions the different stanzas conveyed. Another author, Bacharach, had drawn wheels across the pages and called them prayers of light, and as she strained to understand them, she, too, was flooded with light. When she looked up, she saw that the sun was setting on the horizon.

A Sufi dervish named Djuneyd hid in his cloak and found God in its depths. The great dervish and poet Rumi invited her through the pages of his Masnawi to come to him as she was. A traveler and philosopher, Ibn Al'Arabi, who had written *The Bezels of Wisdom*, set the stone of her heart in a setting that was faithful to its essence.

Later, in the fading light, turning the pages of another book, Sara saw a succession of lizards crossing the width of the book from right to left although there were no illustrations or words that hinted at the presence of reptiles. When she looked away from the book to rest her exhausted eyes she noticed a small lizard crawling across the carpet underneath the window.

She must have shrieked because she heard Ali's soothing voice. "She's harmless, Sara. Her family has been living here as long as the house has been here. They like this room because they can blend into it. Usually, they're quite shy with strangers but the book you're holding always draws them out."

She closed the book and placed it on the floor. "Why does it bring them out?"

"Because it is called *Treatise on the Dragons*," Ali said. "It counsels its readers to live among dragons before calling on the angel of the Lord for redemption."

Her eyes felt heavy. She was dizzy with fatigue. She was about to ask Ali if they could continue later when he said, "You've seen enough, Sara, enough to remember them."

"Yes, yes," she agreed, eager to leave the green room and the green chair.

In the kitchen Ali prepared dinner. When had he boiled the potatoes? Where had the feta cheese, black olives, and the fresh loaf of bread come from? When had he slipped out of the library to make-up the bed behind the stove? She noticed that the narrow space behind the stove was really a cubby hole with a little window facing the hill. She wondered which cabinet with trick doors had held the puffy pillows and the shiny satin quilt that now adorned the bed.

Ali unfolded a chaise longue for Sara to sit in. He served her tea in a narrow-waisted tea glass with two gold bands circling its rim. They sipped their tea quietly in the kitchen in the fading light of the day. Ali said he preferred not to turn on the electricity and Sara agreed with him. They drank tea and talked and ate bread and olives and talked some more as the evening turned into night and the stillness outside the house became a protective cover for them and their stories. Sara told Ali of her need for love and her fear of love. She confessed she felt as if she were meant to do something special on earth, but it wasn't clear to her what that was yet. Ali responded that he, too, felt he was chosen for something special, but that unlike Sara, he didn't have to search the world for it. It was a duty he would fulfill in the same house he was born in, with the help of the library.

"Don't you need anyone in your life, then?" Sara asked.

"Of course I do," said Ali, "love is the only transmuter of the soul. I need love for my soul wisdom to manifest itself."

"Don't you think it's important to love a woman for who she is, instead of what she can do for your soul?"

"I'm not sure I have room for both kinds of love," answered Ali.

"It seems we both have similar fears in love," mused Sara.

"And similar hopes for what love can do for us," said Ali.

"Except that my idea of what love can do is not as clearly defined as yours."

"Neither is mine. Although I can define what I want, I have no idea what I will find once I begin to explore it. Somewhat like the pomegranate," added Ali upon reflection.

"What do you mean, like the pomegranate?"

"There is a Turkish riddle which goes like this: 'I bought one in the market, discovered a thousand at home.' Which means that when you buy a pomegranate, you think you're bringing home a single fruit, something red and lumpy, with a dry peel. But once you crack it open, you have a thousand fleshy seeds, each to be savored slowly, their sweet clear juice to be patiently imbibed. We have a pomegranate tree outside the house."

"On which side?"

"The hill side."

"Can I see it?"

"You can hear it!"

And sure enough Sara heard a branch tapping on the small window of the cubby hole behind the bed. She also heard the rain. A thundershower had started as they talked, and it was coming down with the force of the rains which had made Noah's ark a refuge. Heavy droplets quickly coalesced into thick rivulets on the window. Despite the storm, Sara felt safe in this house, certain that it, too, would float—library, lizards, and all—if there were a deluge and the Marmara sea rose to the top of the island.

Ali said he wanted to make sure the living room windows were properly closed. He asked Sara to come along so she could see another part of the house. They passed through a door beside the door that led to the library. Down a few steps was a large living room with wide windows on both sides. The front stairs of the house were visible from the windows overlooking the sea. They probably led to a door that was connected to the hall at the far end of the living room.

Large white sheets had been draped over the furniture for the winter. There weren't many ornaments on the shelves on the walls except huge sea shells in unusual shapes, some with flaring lips, some with purplish interiors, the conches spinning as they stood still, from a mad central whorl. Several dried starfish of various sizes, their fingers curled in gestures of patience, were dispersed among the sea shells.

"Some of these sea shells are as old as the books in the library," commented Ali. My namesake Ali Effendi, who was a marine customs broker, collected them. It is said that he used to listen to the sounds coming from them as a kind of meditation."

"What did he do with the starfish, then?" asked Sara.

"Contemplated them, I guess, for their shape and their message."

On the walls, in simple wooden frames, were many photographs dating from the middle of the nineteenth century when the first camera became available in Istanbul. As Ali carefully secured all the windows against the rain, Sara examined the photographs. At the turn of the century women had preferred to pose with a book in their hands next to a vase of flowers, whereas men had preferred to pose with crude tennis rackets held across their chests or next to bicycles with massive rubber tires. Some of the men wore fezzes and some were bareheaded. Although most of the women wore European style dresses, quite a few of them had stretched a scarf tightly across their foreheads, knotting it with a fancy knot above an ear, to expertly hide their hair.

Back in the kitchen Sara and Ali approached the bed together, lifting the rose and carnation-patterned satin quilt at the same time, sitting on the pale orange sheet together as though they had slept with each other for many years, and this was just another night in a long union. Ali was attracted to her, and she to him, so they embraced and kissed and touched and sighed with desire. When Sara felt Ali move inside her she knew that she had become his bride, for she had opened herself to his destiny. As waves of sweet warmth spread through her body Sara sensed that her body could be a vehicle for the transmutation of his soul, and her soul, a medium for his dreams.

Afterwards Sara sat up in the bed and listened to the rain. Ali lay quietly, contemplating the framed drawing on the wall across from the bed, placed so that it could be seen best when a person was lying on the bed looking up.

"Do you have any cigarettes?" asked Sara.

Ali was surprised because Sara had not smoked a single cigarette since they met. "There must be a few packages of my grandmother's cigarettes left," he answered, rising.

He rummaged in a small drawer in the cabinet built into the kitchen wall behind the chair where Sara had sat when they had dinner. He found a small flat white cardboard box and handed it to her. There was a line drawing in red of a poppy on the box.

Sara read aloud the brand name. "Gelincik."

"Which means poppy."

"Poppy?"

"Don't, worry, it's regular tobacco."

Sara opened the box of the flattest and thinnest cigarettes she had ever seen.

"It used to be the favorite brand of old ladies like my grandmother," said Ali. "Gelincik also means 'dear bride.' Funny,

I never thought of this meaning before. I guess this brand appealed to women for several reasons."

Ali handed Sara a small bowl to use as an ashtray, and lit her cigarette with a match.

Sara inhaled. The cigarette caught the flame only on one side and burned halfway up.

"You'll be traveling soon," said Ali. "That's what it means."

"Hardly a prophecy," answered Sara. "Of course, I'll be moving on."

Ali appeared hurt by her off-hand remark. He asked her to put out the half-burned cigarette and take another.

When she lit the second cigarette the same thing happened. It caught the flame on the opposite side and again, burned right up to the middle.

"I guess you'll be coming back," said Ali.

This time it was Sara who seemed upset. She stubbed the cigarette in the bowl and said it was best not to smoke anyway.

Sara lay in bed with her fingers laced behind her head staring at the small drawing on the wall. In the moonlight streaming in through the small window, she could see men in oriental kaftans talking to each other in twos. They were bent toward each other as if exchanging conspiratorial whispers. She could almost hear their anxious, hurried exchange. What was the story about? If she only listened better, if she only pretended that she weren't listening, like the man at the centre of the picture whose back was turned to them, then maybe she would hear them. Who were these people with such a compelling story? Maybe Ali knew. As she fell asleep, she resolved to ask him.

I am on a ferry sailing up the Bosphorus. It is a breezy day in October. The sun peeks through the clouds every so often and brightens the earth. I sit outside on a bench at the side of the ferry and watch the shoreline pass by. As the ferry heads north the settlements along the shore appear to be more traditional and further apart. It is obvious that fewer people live in these neighborhoods, and they are less hurried.

I notice people sitting on folding chairs at the edge of the water, watching ferries like the one I am on go by. No one is in a hurry; they seem to enjoy waiting. Waiting is a way of life for them. I feel as though I have traveled backward in time while I've been on the ferry for an hour.

Past Beykoz at a small stop, I decide to leave the ferry. I notice that there is a restaurant right above the water, on an old wharf. They have opened the windows wide, so that the clients are sitting in full sunlight by the edge of the water, right over the water, even as they are sheltered by the roof of the restaurant. I want to experience this, being inside and outside at the same time.

In the restaurant a waiter with a huge scar across his forehead, running from the hairline on one side of his head to the top of his brow on the other side, greets me. He seems to be a man accustomed to waiting. I ask him his name although I am not in the habit of asking waiters their names. He tells me he is called Melek, that it means angel in Turkish. I am surprised to hear a man named Angel. He shows me to a table by the water.

Soon I am joined by the owner of the restaurant, a burly man named Tartar. "Welcome to Tartar's restaurant," he says. I thank him for greeting me. I ask him why he makes Melek wait. Angels should not be kept waiting. Tartar answers that this Angel is no good because he is scarred. "He is not fit to appear in public," Tartar says. "He is lucky I let him wait here until his scar heals."

"Has his scar improved over the years?" I ask. I am surprised by the medical tone of my voice.

"Those kind of scars have never been known to improve," Tartar answers smugly, laughing at my naiveté, and at the Angel's because both Melek and I are hopeful of healings.

I am seized by an urge to persuade Melek to leave this place. He must, he must, I think. A marked Angel is what the world has been waiting for. I am convinced, but Melek is hesitant because he has been told, as have the rest of us, that Angels must be perfect.

I take his hand and bring it to my heart, pressing his hand over my heart, on my breast. Tartar, who is watching us from where he is sitting behind the cash register, thinks we are getting it on, the naive tourist and his hapless waiter.

I keep Melek's hand on my heart. He sits across from me. I watch the scar on his forehead shrink and then diminish. We will leave together, before nightfall. Melek assures me there is one last ferry. I believe him. I have to believe him.

In the morning, while they were still in bed, drowsy with sleep, Sara recounted her dream. Ali held her hand and kissed her on her eyebrows.

"Sara," he said, "you have seen the scarred messiah. He was called Melek in your dream which means you met him in his soul form. He was a waiter in your dream because he has been waiting for a long time. The Messiah will return soon because the world needs him. He has been maligned because he wanted to unify the opposites in the world so that he could help the world abandon its commitment to opposition. When he was alive he turned Jews into Muslims, and Christians and Muslims into

Jews. Many people believed in him when he first walked the earth, but there were also many who denied his message and tried to suppress it. They called him the false messiah, that's why you saw him as a scarred man. A maligned man is a scarred man. Through his example we will all learn to be messiahs and learn the importance of wandering as well as of waiting. We will accept our scars and exalt them as our identifying marks."

"Why was I given this dream?" asked Sara.

"His wife was also called Sara."

"And why here?"

"Because his books are here, in my library, and I have been waiting here for him as well."

"Why did I see him by the water?"

"Because he will come back from the sea, from the other shore where he has been exiled. That is why those who still believe in him go to the shore daily to greet him, to remind him that he is welcome back."

"I don't know what to do with all this," answered Sara. "I was only traveling. This is what most young women my age in North America do. They go abroad to find themselves. I don't know what to make of this, Ali."

Ali kissed her eyebrows again. "Don't worry, Sara," he said, gently. "You can take your time. You have just as much right as everybody else to take your time with this story."

He rose and went to the cabinet where he had stored his grandmother's cigarettes. He opened another drawer and pulled out another cardboard box. From the box he extracted a silver ring with a brownish red stone. He gave it to Sara.

"Please take this," he said. "It's meant for you." Sara slipped the ring on her ring finger. It fit perfectly. There was a large S carved into the red stone, but it was so masterfully done that it seemed to be part of a continuous design, flowing from the ends of the vine engraved into the silver band.

Sara gasped. "Thank you! Are you sure? It looks like an antique."

"It is. It was Salih Effendi's ring."

"The same Salih Effendi that was your namesake Ali Effendi's best friend?"

"That's right."

"The man who came from Spain?"

"Yes, but this is the ring he had made for himself when he decided to settle in Istanbul. The stone is called carnelian or chalcedony, which derives its name from an ancient settlement, perhaps the first one on the Bosphorus, called Chalcedon. This is the stone of that city and it can heal. It is a mystical stone that will help you remember the wisdom of the ancients and hear their stories."

Sara turned the ring around her finger. She liked the feel of the vine engraved into the band. She rotated the ring again. She rubbed the S on the stone with the middle finger of her left hand and thought of her name. She felt as though she were surrounded by women who had shared her name since the beginning of time. She turned the ring again and touched the vine that circled the band. She took a deep breath. A rush of air more forceful than what she had inhaled coursed through her. The morning light shone on her through the cubby hole window. She held the ring to the light and listened to the whispers that always ride a stream of light, old whispers that told a story that was hers and Ali's and others', and of much, much more.

TWO

By Our Wanderings We Seek

THE MAN INSPECTING typefaces in Rabbi Menasseh ben Israel's printing shop had recently arrived from Spain. He had been sent by the rector of the University of Alcala to oversee the printing of a pamphlet on the interpretation of the diagnostic methods of the plague as prescribed in Leviticus, for use in a theology seminar. When he impulsively confessed to the rabbi that he, too, was a son of Israel, the rabbi, who had gotten into trouble with the agents of the Inquisition in the past, refrained from flinging up his arms with joy at this announcement that another Jew had returned to the fold. "Praised be the Lord, Adonai, for the Lord is great," he said simply.

Samuel repeated his declaration. Then, he told the rabbi: "I am a son of Israel, of the tribe of Levi. That much I know for sure, but not much more, for these were the last words my father told me before he was taken away, along with my mother and my two older brothers and sister, by the guards of the Inquisition. We were living in the town of Bragança. I was six years old and escaped notice because my birth had not been properly regis-tered. I learned more later from the Jesuit monks who adopted me when they found me wandering in the streets after my family was taken away."

"The monks investigated my origins and told me that I had been a gift of God to them since my family seemed to have perished without a trace from the face of the earth. As they had saved me from certain starvation of the body as well as of the soul by taking me under their wing, they believed that I would save others from the manifold dreads of the spirit. Therefore, they gave me the name Salvador. I believe, however, that I was of the family of Gonçalves because I later ascertained that a family similar to mine by that name perished in the auto-da-fé of Coimbra in 1632."

"You must realize," Samuel continued, "that I do not know how to be a good Jew, but in the deepest recesses of my heart I have been a follower of the Mosaic precepts. I have observed the Sabbath as much as I could, retiring for prayer into the chapel on the Holy Day, fasting as much as I was able to from the forbidden meats and fowl without attracting attention, and have never uttered the name of the Lord in vain. I have tried to serve my Jewish brethren well in my capacity as a Jesuit monk, assisting them whenever I could, ensuring their safe passage when I observed them leaving my town, or by arranging for them to be served proper food in the dungeons of the Inquisition, and to be attended by physicians when they suffered from the effects of torture and interrogation. I may not be able to prove to you that I am of pure Jewish blood, but I can easily prove that I am of pure Jewish heart if you admit me to your bosom, here in Amsterdam."

Samuel had then been made welcome by the rabbi who was won over by his declaration. The rabbi hastened to make Samuel's situation clear to the community of Jews, whose elders did not inquire deeply about his beliefs before he joined them, but resolved to teach him the laws of Moses properly, as soon as possible, so that, Samuel, too, could be blessed daily by them.

Samuel Salvador took to their teachings like a fish to water, revelling in the continuity of that mighty stream of tradition as if his nature had finally found its true habitat. He attended the Portuguese synagogue for morning prayers daily and he was to be found there all day every Sabbath. He took to wearing his prayer shawl with the same meticulous care he had once worn his monk's cowl in the monastery in Spain. He read the Old Testament in Hebrew now, delighting in discussing the correspondences to, and the deviations from the Latin text he had studied so ardently throughout his youth. He found himself embraced with familial love for the first time in his life. He was frequently invited to the homes of his Jewish brethren where he charmed his hosts and hostesses with his gracious good manners and his learned discussions of Iberian culture and politics and his eagerness to learn about the free life in the Low Countries.

At the end of his first year in Amsterdam, Samuel was given a job teaching secular subjects at the local Talmud Torah where, for the next three years, he distinguished himself with his dedication to his pupils, especially those who were slow to learn their sums, or faltered in their conjugation of Latin verbs. He lived penuriously in a room attached to the school whose only window looked into the courtyard of the Lazaretto where beggars and lepers with infested sores quietly gathered in the evenings after a day of sounding their clappers in the alleys of Amsterdam, announcing their arrival to all who feared contact with them and the effluvia of their ailments.

After his duties in the classroom were finished and the last of the students who needed private tutoring had gone home, Samuel sat in his small room with a woolen blanket over his shoulders, warming his tired feet over a brazier, and a quilt pulled over his knees to keep the warmth of the coals close to his body. That he had escaped death by burning at an auto-da-fé like the rest of his family occurred to him whenever he warmed his body like this in Amsterdam. He checked the coals more often than necessary because he didn't want to challenge fate by disrespecting fire.

Often he stared impassively at the courtyard, watching the mendicants exchange pleasantries among themselves, their deformed and misshaped bodies relaxed in the company of others who were similarly cursed. An easy familiarity existed among the lepers. Samuel noted how, with perceptible swiftness every evening, they shed their oddly belligerent gait and the sarcastic expressions on what was left of their scarred faces once they stepped through the gate of the Lazaretto.

Although Samuel was of fair appearance, he too, had carried an armour of defensiveness throughout his life. At the Jesuit monastery in his hometown of Bragança, he had remained tense even when playing tag with the other young wards at recess. Inside the cloistered courtyard there was little incentive for gaiety under the watchful eyes of the friars. Occasionally, as he ran around the only tree in the courtyard, a stately oak which was the boys' natural base in games of tag, he had perceived the freedom that was promised to him in his young muscles.

When he touched the tree to declare his safety from the boy who was "it," he had felt released from the religious shackles that bound him. In those moments it had seemed to Samuel that his friends' eyes shone brighter than the jewels over the blessed Mary's crown in the chapel, and that the spring in their calf muscles was forceful enough to catapult them over the walls of the monastery into the streets of their town to happily scatter in all directions toward points of the earth as yet uncharted by the Jesuits.

When the lepers heard the sonorous peals of the bell signalling their dinner of herring soup and bread was to be served, they stepped through the door of the institution in an orderly file, the sickliest and therefore slowest of them waiting patiently until the others had crossed the threshold underneath the gable adorned with a large palmette relief. The lepers had no reason to hurry or to shove one another, for each of them was guaranteed respite from his misery at the end of the day with dinner and a cot. In keeping with the fairness of Calvinist precepts, they were also certain of a helping of pleasure in addition to their basic nourishment. For an hour after dinner the lepers smoked the spiced tobacco that was distributed evenly among them.

Although he could no longer observe them inside the dining hall, Samuel continued watching the orange glow of their lit pipes on the dark window, his heart startling him with its joy, as if he had peered inside a Spanish pomegranate on a sunny day. The chill of his loneliness became more acute then despite the warmth of the brazier at his feet, and Samuel yearned for the company of Alonzo Melami, his confidante during his years in the Jesuit monastery.

Alonzo Melami was a foundling like himself, but of Moorish origin. The two boys had studied the Catholic liturgy together, quizzed each other on their lessons before examinations, served at the altar together on Sundays, and dreamt together of traveling on church missions. Time and destiny had separated them, however, and Samuel had lost track of Alonzo's travels a few years after he came to the University of Alcala for his studies. He guessed at Alonzo's whereabouts from bits of gossip. Although many of their friends had volunteered for missions in the New World, in Mexico, Alonzo had most probably settled in the Levant at a Jesuit outpost in Syria or Jerusalem, where his aptitude for the Arabic language would have served his mission well.

Samuel had taken the more academic route by studying theology, medicine, and law. Although innately intelligent, he had lacked the tenacity and stubbornness necessary to become a Jesuit missionary. He was channelled into scholarly studies by the friars who had been anxious to keep a close watch on him to ensure that he would not relapse. Throughout his years at the seminary, his newness to Christianity had never been mentioned, but Samuel knew that the Catholic administrators were suspicious of foundlings like himself, New Christians in the truest sense, who could revert to the practices of their bloodline in a moment of weakness.

Samuel had always been aware of his uneasy acceptance by the Jesuits. The irony of his Christian name never failed to amuse him. He often wondered if he was destined to be a Saviour of the relapsed, or of himself? Was he the weak link in a mighty chain who would always require salvation by others with stronger convictions?

If only Alonzo were here with him in Amsterdam. They would have been able to debate and argue the theological points which the rabbis advocated. Was the spirit transcendent; was it true that Jesus was only a man of flesh and bones like any other mortal? Why was Moses deemed the only lawgiver on earth when God had also sent other prophets to speak in other languages besides Hebrew for Him? Didn't the appearance of other prophets throughout history refute the claim of the rabbis that the laws of Moses were perfect and immutable? And what balderdash was the assertion of the Talmudic sages that the dead who had been pious in their lifetime are rolled along underground passages from Europe to Palestine for resurrection!

If Alonzo could now be sitting with him in this room, Samuel felt he would not feel as lonely as he did, under the assault of his suspicions. He had arrived where he had hoped he would safely anchor his soul, but his soul was still restless and it frightened him to admit this at nightfall. The thud of a pail hitting the stone wall at the edge of the canal aroused him from his thoughts. He noted with annoyance that it was the servant girl Geertje from the residence adjoining the Lazaretto, emptying her pail of dirty water and refuse into the canal. All was not well in this city. He no longer believed Amsterdam was heaven on earth. There were cheats everywhere. Geertje, for example, refused to obey the city ordinances and blithely blamed the lepers every time the night guards spotted her refuse on the canal.

Samuel rose from his seat beside the window, carefully covered the cinders in the brazier with ash to smother them, and walked toward his bed. He took off his coat, his jacket and pants, but left on his undergarments and his wool socks. He neatly piled the garments he had taken off on a chair that stood at the foot of his bed. He reached for the old sweater which he kept folded in a small niche in the wall behind the chair, and slipped it over his undergarments. He rearranged his wool cap snugly over his ears. Then he spread the woolen blanket which he had draped over his shoulders through the evening on his bed. It would help trap the warmth of the down quilt underneath it. Before he slipped under the covers, he checked to see that his pitcher of water was within arm's reach, but not too close, in case he thrashed about during a fitful dream. He absentmindedly pressed together the few bound volumes on the shelf over his bed as if he were tucking them in for the night. Last, he blew out the candle on his bedside table.

He was offered a white envelope. "Take it," said his grammar teacher, Senhor Manoel Torcato, his beady eyes glowing with urgency. But it was his lips which stood out most in his narrow sallow face. They were always as red as if he had just taken a swig from the wine bottle he kept hidden in the lower drawer of his massive wooden desk. For a man who had recited short passages from a Latin gradus to his young charges all his life, Senhor Torcato's lips were unnaturally alive, as if much more than cumbersome verbs depended upon them for enunciation.

Senhor Torcato's lips had never failed to startle Samuel when he glanced upon them for the first time each morning. It did not matter that he had watched them move around vowels and clam shut with consonants throughout the previous school day. Each morning their carmine tumescence discharged invisible taunts, challenging Samuel to wipe the seeds of sleep from his eyes and clear his throat to begin speaking.

"A good Jesuit must know how to persuade, how to cajole and chide, and how to instill the fear of Satan and Hell," lectured Senhor Torcato, his voice pitched high for Satan, yet falling to a barely audible hiss at Hell. All the while, his rubious lips insinuated the wordless temptations of demons.

"Good day, Senhor Torcato."

"Go on, go on, what are you waiting for?" asked Senhor Torcato.

"Open the envelope."

Samuel's fingers trembled as he picked up the square envelope which was in fact a large manuscript sheet whose four corners had been evenly folded over the side that bore the writing. A red wax seal affixed the four flaps together where they met at the centre. When he held the envelope up to the light to see if he could make out the writing on the other side, Samuel noticed the large S that had been stamped on the seal. The person who had sealed the document had been hasty and dripped a large quantity of wax. He had stamped the S with a signet ring before wiping out the excess wax. Consequently, the wax had rolled over the two curves of the letter, blurring its contours.

"What is the S for?" asked Samuel, hesitantly.

"Open it, it is meant for you," hissed Senhor Torcato. "Don't you see it is your own signature, that huge S? S for Samuel and S for Salvador. Yours is a name that encourages double attention because it may be doubly overlooked."

"I have nothing to do with this letter," Samuel insisted. "In any case, I have never owned a signet ring."

"S is also for secret," snapped Senhor Torcato. "You have kept this document a secret from yourself until now, because you were not ready to study it."

Samuel could not dispute the logic of these words. He lifted the wax from the centre of the envelope with the nail of his little finger. He was surprised when the wax peeled off easily. He noticed that the edges of the two adjacent flaps of the envelope which met in a diagonal line from the left corner towards the centre were jagged. He wondered if the letter had been written on a leaf which had been ripped hastily from a bound volume.

Senhor Torcato pointed his fleshy lips at Samuel. It occurred to Samuel that Senhor Torcato's lips were of the same colour as the wax seal. Perhaps this was a terrible ruse.

"Read it." ordered Senhor Torcato. "Aloud!"

The room darkened as if the sun had been pulled out of the sky by an invisible cord. Samuel was going to protest that there was not enough light in the room, when he noticed the page gleamed by itself. Indeed, it was his own handwriting, from when he was still a young schoolboy in the monastery in Bragança. He recognized the boyish flourish of the L with which he had started the title: "Lingua".

"Lingua, the tongue," he read aloud.

"Go on!" snapped Senhor Torcato.

Samuel recognized the essay now. It had been a long time since he had laid eyes on it. He had been required to copy it from a codicil to the grammar textbook they had used in his beginners' Latin class. He had copied it as a final assignment and written an explanation in his own words in Portuguese. The essay was the Latin rendition of an Aesop fable about "the tongue." His portion of the fable had been the section where the slave is examined by his master after the slave serves a tongue dish at a banquet in honour of the city's highest officials and later, hastily offers the remnants as lunch to a group of beggars who have called on the door of his master's establishment. The infuriated master requires an explanation from his wise slave who has never before betrayed his trust or behaved in a contrary manner. "What is the meaning of your contradictory actions?" the master asks. "For you have served the same item both when I asked for a delicacy and for a simple handout."

The slave dutifully answers that the tongue is capable of satisfying many functions. It may turn a compliment to please the most refined company and yet nourish the lowliest of humans. "How it is served, to whom, and by whom is the key," the slave replies. His master is satisfied with the explanation and is so pleased that he grants the slave his freedom instead of punishing him with death.

Samuel was anxious to discern Senhor Torcato's reaction to the contents of the envelope. Would he be punished now? Would this secret document and its seditious lesson endanger *his* life as it had once endangered the life of the slave?

Samuel noted with astonishment that he and his teacher were now seated alone at the large table in the refectory of the orphanage. Senhor Torcato was busy spooning noodles into his mouth from a large silver tureen shaped like Noah's ark. He encouraged Samuel to help himself from the same abundant source. Samuel reached for a spoon that had been conveniently placed at his side. He heard someone in the kitchen transferring more noodles into another container with a swoosh.

As he picked up the spoon, Samuel noticed that his arm was bare. When he anxiously glanced at his chest, he saw that he was totally bereft of clothing. "Jesus," he thought, "My Lord, why have you exposed me so to my teacher?"

Senhor Torcato chuckled as if he had read Samuel's mind. "Eat," he urged. "Use that tongue well. Eat and enjoy your nakedness, for it is not a shame to lay your body bare. From the nakedness of your body will follow the nakedness of your heart and then, your soul. Your tongue will nourish you well along the way. Eat, so you may do away with all covers."

Samuel woke up to find that he had kicked off his quilt and blanket. He pulled them back over his body and took a swig from his pitcher before falling asleep again.

"Confess, confess," hissed a burly man through the slit in the hood that concealed his head, "admit your betrayal."

"Admit what?" Samuel asked, or wanted to ask, for his tongue was too pained to articulate the question. His tongue lay still and swollen in his mouth, too heavy with pain to admit that he had been a Judaizer in the midst of the faithful who had sheltered him from starvation and cold when he was a foundling without a name on the alleys of Bragança.

"I have never erred in my devotions," protested Samuel.

"What did you say?" asked the torturer through the slit in the hood over his mouth. "Speak up."

"Oh please, senor, please, let me speak, for I cannot speak with my tongue in your grip," answered Samuel, but no words issued from his lips.

"Admit your intentions," hissed the man, yanking the rope attached to the pulleys over the torture rack. Samuel's head twitched violently despite the garrote that kept his neck pinned to the board.

Samuel wondered why his tongue had not been torn off yet. "Oh, sir, I have done nothing wrong. I have kept my mouth shut all my life." Samuel's saliva gurgled in his throat as he tried to swallow. "Please señor please, either pull a little harder so that I may surrender my tongue or let me go. Forgive me for all that you say I have done, although I swear I have no memory of any of it."

The torturer tugged at the cord that tightened the contraption. Samuel was ready to give up his tongue if it meant that the torture would stop. The pull on his tongue hurt more than the wresting of his joints or the pressure of the garrote on his neck. "Let it be ripped and separated from me," he thought, "it is of no use to me now. It cannot save me anymore, for it cannot serve my intellect. Perhaps, I will fare better as a mute," he speculated in agony. "If I am allowed to live."

Samuel woke up in the narrow bed in the room attached to the schoolhouse. He was relieved to see that dawn had already broken. His body was drenched with sweat. His sheets were thoroughly soaked, as were his underwear and nightshirt. He removed his wool cap and flung it across the room. He would rise and go for a walk along the canals before starting the school day. A brisk walk usually cleared his head and helped heal the pains in his joints. He sat up in his bed and drank lustily from the pitcher.

At the DaCosta household Samuel was expected to teach Latin, basic and advanced arithmetic, and dancing. The last requirement had struck him as absurd the first time it was mentioned to him by his employer, and he had protested, arguing that he had lived all his life in an orphanage, a monastery, and a Jesuit college; always celibate, and never in the company of women. "Dancing was an activity enjoyed by others. The most I could do was watch, and that was not possible very often, either. Please understand, Señor Jeronimo Da Costa, as Jesuits, we were kept apart from the kind of people who danced. In fact, we were taught to condemn them."

Señor DaCosta was adamant. "Samuel," he argued, "you have come to Amsterdam and started a new life as a Jew, to live far from the fetters and habits of your old existence. Dancing is an art you must teach yourself if you wish to live among us. If you are required to teach it to your students, you will be compelled to learn it yourself."

Samuel had cringed at the idea. He considered it preposterous that a man his age, forty years old, already greying at the temples, balding, a celibate man who had never come close to kissing a woman, was expected to dance with boys. He needed the new job, however. He could not refuse the opportunity of bettering himself and gaining a measure of financial independence.

His salary at the Talmud Torah had been recently reduced due to the economic crises afflicting the Jewish community. Fewer people were able to pay the charity dues that they had promised. The payments that had been collected were distributed to the rising numbers of poor Jews both among the Spanish Jews and among the recently arrived German Jews for their pressing needs of food, medicine, and shelter.

Samuel accepted the employment offer with the proviso that until he learned how to dance (he promised to pay for his own dancing classes), he would be held exempt from teaching dance. He offered to conduct walks along the Amstel river with his charges as a substitute course. "They will get their exercise, certainly more than if they were dancing indoors," he argued. "In addition, we will discuss philosophical matters and comment upon the social situations that we observe. In this way, your children will acquire a taste for philosophy. This is certainly not a novel method. You must have heard about the Greek philosophers who taught their students in this manner."

Although a successful merchant, Jeronimo DaCosta was not well-versed in either philosophy or history. He was too shrewd a man to admit his ignorance in public and as he customarily did in such circumstances, he refrained from pressing the issue and nodded in agreement.

Samuel was assigned a well-lighted and spacious room in the DaCosta household on the third floor overlooking the Herengracht canal. At his insistence, the room was furnished with only the functional necessities and stripped of the useless knickknacks such as the imported ornamental porcelain plates, glass bibelots, and collections of sea shells with which wealthy merchants liked to adorn their houses.

Within a few days of settling into his new room and his new bed Samuel could no longer deny how difficult he found it to embrace the values of the wealthy Jews who took an interest in his welfare. He refrained from making any statements in public lest his employer and patron sense his dissatisfaction. His previous life had taught him well how to suppress his private emotions behind a veneer of stoicism and scholarly rhetoric, and he admitted, not without some acrimony, that he must continue doing the same among those of his own blood.

He was aware that their interest in him was not purely altruistic; they valued his academic credentials and his superior knowledge of Latin and saw in him a worthy teacher for the younger generation. He was also aware that his life story aroused the sympathy of the Jewish mothers who noticed how, at heart, he had remained an insecure orphan who felt awkward in social situations although to all outward appearances he was a middle aged man.

They noticed the gleam of gratitude in his eyes for the simplest acts of kindness and forgave his reluctance to converse with them, attributing his unsociable behaviour to his boyish naivete regarding the rules of society. His peers reasoned that he could be restored to their company with a dose of friendly guidance. His unwillingness to share his thoughts only nourished their illusions. Little did they guess that he was reluctant to be changed by them.

With his young charges, on the other hand, he was buoyant, witty, and lighthearted. In the classroom at the DaCosta mansion, he often resorted to jokes to get his points across. He taught the boys Latin tongue twisters, imitated his own Latin teacher at the monastery, Senhor Torcato, for comic effect, pursing his lips and exclaiming "calavernis, coques!" ("skulls! polls!") when the boys offered outlandish responses to his questions.

Through Samuel Salvador, the boys could glimpse the landscape and customs of Spain and Portugal, the countries their fathers and grandfathers had fled in haste. When Samuel described Portugal or Spain a new climate took hold in the classroom so that a bright sun broke through the leaden clouds of the Amsterdam sky and the sweet smell of orange and lemon blossoms wafted through the window. The sound of the steady rain beating against the roof tiles and the copper drainage pipes abated and they heard the raspy rustle of the leathery leaves of olive trees in the breeze instead. Samuel described the even rows of olive trees in the groves so vividly that the boys imagined themselves walking there, reaching up to pluck the black fruit from the silvery green branches overhead. He described the chestnuts and the pomegranates, the quinces and apricots, in bloom as in maturity, and the herbs and flowers particular to the southern climates. He filled their hearts with longing so that they soon asked him how they could return to these countries, undetected, if only to see with their own eyes the wondrous sights he described.

Samuel dissuaded them from returning. He told them that even though the countryside was welcoming, the people were not. He told them that those who dared travel as Jews in Spain or Portugal would be subject to utter degradation, perhaps starvation, begging for a slice of dry bread and a jug of water from the country folk who would throw stones to deter them and chase them out of their towns. If they were foolish enough to think they could disguise themselves as Christians by wearing Christian robes and hanging a cross from their necks, they would ultimately be found out because they were circumcised. "No man has been capable of fastening that piece back," he said glumly. "Then you will be at the mercy of the Inquisition who will think nothing of throwing you into a rat-infested dungeon for a dozen years before questioning you, and your first sight of the sky after that may well be your last, as you are paraded in the street on your way to the stake, wearing a sambenito depicting devils throwing heretics like yourself into the fires of hell."

"No," Samuel concluded with a sigh, "you *don't* want to go back. Believe me."

The boys did not believe him because it was obvious to them that Samuel did not think his life in Amsterdam was much better. Because they could not understand why Samuel did not appreciate his life in Amsterdam as he should, because he did not proclaim, like the other newcomers, "Bless Adonai, for my salvation and safe delivery to these lands of freedom," the boys suspected that he kept the truth from them. Samuel must know a secret method for living well in Spain, they thought, and believed it was a matter of time before Samuel returned to the sunny land of olives and lemons.

Samuel was unable to find a dance master to teach him the courante, the sarabande, or the new rage of the time, the minuet. He had not tried hard. Most of what he knew he had learned from books he reasoned, and bought a dance manual for half a guilder at a book shop on Harlemmerstraat. He started by practicing the steps for the courante, which seemed to him to be the easiest because it was more theatre than dance. He followed the detailed instructions to mimic polishing his shoes, arranging his shirt, and wringing his hands in agony, all to make himself more desirable to the imaginary ladies who had supposedly just refused his amorous advances. But when he caught sight of himself in the oval mirror above the washstand, his face contorted, his hair disheveled, his eyes glaring with intense concentration, he cried aloud in frustration.

"Fool," he hissed at himself. "Stupid old fool. Who are you? A Jesuit who became Jewish in Amsterdam to become the nanny of spoiled boys. Just look at yourself, you old wretch. Trying so hard to keep your stupid job by what, by trying to dance like a dandy! Have you lost all reason, you fool?"

He sat down in the stiff-backed armchair at the corner of his room, his chest heaving with rage and exhaustion. He was surprised to feel salty tears welling in his eyes. It had been a long time since he had last cried. He had learned very early on not to cry, for it was useless, absolutely useless. He could not afford the luxury of crying in the orphanage and he could not afford it now in Amsterdam. "What is the use of it," he asked himself again, gritting his teeth, and noticed that he was sobbing now, like a helpless woman.

He remembered the dances he had witnessed in Portugal, in the town of his birth, Bragança. The townspeople danced the folia with drunken fury at the carnivals, castanets clapping so fast that the hands holding them became blurred, the fingers snapping open and shut like vicious birds pecking at imaginary grains in the air. The men dressed up as women, and the women in turn dressed up as men. Some of them carried masked effigies on their shoulders so that the effect was of double duplicity. Which was the true head, which the true gender, it was impossible to tell. Who was the woman and who the man, who could impregnate the other; in the end, it didn't matter in that frenzy.

It was madness, truly madness, that dance. But at least they acknowledged it and expressed it, and called it by a name that described it honestly. No one had pretensions that it was otherwise. None of the false pretenses that he had to exhibit here in Amsterdam were required there. Despite their cruelty and their rudeness, the people were alive there.

"I'm fed up," Samuel moaned, "I'm fed up with living under false pretenses." He doubled over on the chair and rested his head on his crossed arms. As soon as he said this, another voice inside of him, the voice of reason and determination, the strongest voice inside of him of tenaciousness and survival, reminded him: "You cannot return there Samuel," it said. "You will be persecuted."

"I can't live here either," said Samuel, aloud.

"Here, your ordeal is different. You won't be judged for who you are."

"But I am not like them," Samuel countered.

"You are not so unlike them, either," responded the voice. "A few adjustments in your manners will accomplish the task quite nicely. You'll see, it can only get better from now on. Now, dry your tears, wash your face. Take a deep breath, and stop fretting about dancing."

"Yes, yes," Samuel agreed, "dancing makes me ill. If I could get out of this one obligation, perhaps I would feel better."
"Take the boys out for a walk everyday, like you said you would when you were hired," said the voice. "Señor DaCosta might change his mind about the dance requirement if the boys' walks are instructional."

Samuel and the boys walked in either of two directions, both of which led them to the outskirts of the city. On most days, they took the shorter route. They walked down the Breestraat to the city wall at St. Anthoniespoort. Once they crossed the bridge over the canal outside the gate, they were in the country. It was a pleasant trek. Ash, elder, and elm trees lined the inland side of the road and there was marsh grass and willows by the dike side. Bell flowers and myrtle seemed to bloom year-round. They frequently sighted purple herons and warblers in the marsh grass. The Zuiderzee stretched calm and flat along the side of the road to the village of Diemen. Sometimes a mother duck and her ducklings followed Samuel and his charges, paddling purposefully on the still water until a bend in the road, disappearing unexpectedly in a clump of reeds.

Samuel and his students often encountered peasants from the village carrying farm produce in their large flat baskets. On their way back to the city they saw the same peasants with their empty baskets, walking purposefully as poor people will walk when they carry unaccustomed wealth on their person. Some were drunkards who spent the few stuivers they had earned that day from a sale of eggs or milk or butter on gin or ale at the numerous taverns found all over Amsterdam, especially in the fish market district. If Samuel noted a drunkard weaving toward him and the boys on the path, he cordially nodded and greeted the man, but quickly drew the boys close to him like a mother hen protecting its chicks. He distracted his students by pointing at a barge in the distance bearing a pile of timber or a particularly large spotted cow munching lazily on a meadow by the side of the road.

His students, the brothers Daniel and Jacob DaCosta and their maternal cousins, Isaac Nassi and Joseph Prado were well-fed, well-dressed patrician boys; but like all boys in that difficult, unpredictable time between childhood and adulthood they were often unruly, prone equally to fits of vigour and moodiness. Their arguments with each other, whether about their lessons or financial matters which they practiced discussing with the air of grownups, were polite and measured. In matters of love and sex, however, they could be crude and mean.

Their meanness extended to Samuel as well. They sensed Samuel's reluctance to associate with women and teased him mercilessly about this. They intimated that their aunt Judith DaCosta, a large sad-eyed woman in her late thirties was a good candidate for his affections. Samuel had no interest in this childless widow who, ten years after the death of her husband, still sighed deeply whenever she mentioned his name. The man had been a merchant in the West Indies Trade Company with no particular talents except to waste the family fortune. Samuel suspected that the DaCostas were secretly relieved that he had perished in a shipwreck.

"Don't you see how shy she is whenever she is around you, Señor Salvador," Joseph Prado would start, nudging his cousin, Isaac Nassi to join in.

"Yes, but the other evening, when she excused herself to retire after dinner, she waited around. You must have noticed it, didn't you, Señor Salvador?"

"No I didn't," responded Samuel. "What about it?"

"She only pretended she was tired. She would have stayed with us longer if you had asked her."

"She knows she is welcome to remain with us. It is not up to me to tell her what she should do. She is a grown-up woman."

"Ah, but she looked at you for a long time before she left the room," insisted Joseph. "She likes you, Señor Salvador. I heard it with my own ears."

"What did you hear, Joseph?"

"When you were in your room yesterday afternoon, and our geography tutor Señor Rodrigues was leaving the house, my aunt commented that perhaps Señor Rodrigues should become more friendly with you since you are such a pleasant man and rather lonely."

"So what is so unusual about that?

"My aunt said it so loudly that she wanted our aunt Rachel to hear it, not only Señor Rodrigues."

"She must have spoken loudly because you boys have certainly heard it all," said Samuel, exasperated. "We should hurry back home," he said, trying to change the course of the conversation "The sky is getting darker by the minute. It looks like rain."

The boys were not willing to yield so soon. Once they were captivated by a subject they were relentless. The DaCosta brothers, Daniel and Jacob also joined in. "You would make a good uncle for us," Daniel, the older one, said.

"Yes, you would," concurred Jacob. "Then you'd have to see us more often."

"Or maybe less," suggested Daniel, "if you and aunt Judith move to another house."

"But you'd still tell us stories about Spain, wouldn't you?" asked Jacob childishly.

Daniel wasn't ready to change the topic. "What do you say,

Isaac, would Señor Salvador mind sharing aunt Judith's bedroom? Her bed is small, but the room is large enough."

Samuel was furious. He wanted to lash out and slap Daniel for his insolence, but he reminded himself he was the employee of the boy's father. He could barely contain himself. "Enough," he said curtly. "My life is not a topic for public discussion."

"What is, then?" asked Isaac.

"What do you suggest?" countered Samuel.

"Jesus, tell us about Jesus," said Isaac, egging him on, because he sensed they still had the upper hand. "We all know about Jesus, the baby boy, and Jesus, the young man, but who was the father?"

Samuel didn't reply. Although a professed Jew, he was uncomfortable with the Judaic interpretation of Jesus and his birth. He felt odd, out of place with the boys who were of his own blood, but who were testing him now as if he were a Gentile. The boys would never dare approach the subject with a Gentile because they knew that discussing religious matters with a Gentile was expressly forbidden. An innocent remark about God, Jesus, or simply the state of disrepair of a Church building could get a Jew into big trouble, not just one Jew, but the whole community of Jews. The boys had this admonishment drummed into them from the time they could say their name.

"Who was the father, Señor Salvador?" repeated Jacob.

Samuel felt the question penetrate his own heart. Who was his father? Who was anybody's father, for that matter? "You know the answer, Jacob. What are you trying to ask, now? Be more clear."

"We know that the father was a man, but why do the Gentiles insist it was the Holy Ghost?"

"Because they believe that Jesus was born to a virgin mother."

"Can a woman be a virgin and a mother at the same time,

Señor Salvador?" asked Isaac, with his eyes fixed on a pair of buxom Dutch girls walking toward them on the path, swinging their large flat baskets.

The girls giggled loudly when they saw that Isaac was watching them. Señor Salvador with his wide brimmed hat and the well-dressed boys were a curiosity for them away from the heart of the city.

"In the case of Virgin Mary it was possible," answered Samuel calmly.

"How? If not before the birth of Jesus, she would have lost her virginity while she was giving birth to Jesus," insisted Isaac.

"A woman does not lose her virginity when she is giving birth," said Samuel, and immediately regretted how he had formulated his response. He realized he had given the boys further ammunition.

"How does a woman get pregnant, Señor Salvador?" asked Daniel.

The older boys exchanged knowing looks. Samuel felt the urge to leave the boys there and run away once and for all from his life and duties in Amsterdam.

He clicked his tongue with exasperation, and shook his head. When he stared ahead at the road, unsure of what to do next, he saw a mare, bolting ahead of a team of horses hitched to a cart. A man, standing upright in the cart, was flailing his arms wildly. Samuel had just enough time to grab Daniel and Isaac who were walking close to him and to yell at Joseph and Jacob to throw themselves on the tall grass over the dike.

The mare, the team of horses and the excited man were gone in a flash. The boys were stunned, unable to rise from the ground where they had flung themselves. Samuel realized he was still holding Daniel and Isaac in his arms. When he released his grip, he heard Daniel sniffling, trying to stifle his fear. Isaac stared silently at the disappearing carriage.

"You all saw how the mare was running?" asked Samuel.

"Yes," answered Daniel, between sobs.

"You saw how wild the stallions behind it were?" asked Samuel.

"Yes," said Daniel, again. The other boys were silent.

"Well, if a strong wind were blowing from behind, and if a bit of semen as little as a drop of spittle was flung ahead of the stallions, and if it entered the mare who was running ahead of the stallions, the mare could get pregnant."

"That would be a miracle," said Jacob from where he was still sitting on the grass, leaning on his elbows.

"It certainly would be," agreed Samuel. "Just as Jesus was a miracle."

Samuel knew he had won. He had beat the boys at their own game.

The boys were aghast. Although they were not Gentiles, they knew that what Samuel had just told them was blasphemous. What other heretical thoughts had he instilled in their young minds without them realizing? They walked home quietly, careful not to engage Samuel in further conversation.

Back at the DaCosta residence, believing nothing too unusual had happened that afternoon, Samuel retired to his room without engaging in polite chatter with Ruth DaCosta who led the exhausted boys to the kitchen for hot tea and butter cookies. Lying on his bed, fully clothed, Samuel listened to the rain that had been threatening to break all afternoon. Large raindrops beat insistently against the lead casings of the window. He felt as if the sky was sending a downpour of pebbles to awaken him from his illusions, urging him to wake up, heed his own thoughts and follow his own desires.

"Should I try to stay with them," he asked himself. "What type of life awaits me here, with these people?"

He acknowledged that it would become harder as time passed, for him to remain a bachelor. The Jewish people put great stock on marriage and the establishment of families. Who could he marry? Did he want to become a father? It was obvious from the boys' discussion that afternoon, that the DaCosta family remarked on his condition and discussed his future among themselves. Maybe for another man this would be a golden opportunity to enter the mainstream of Jewish life by becoming attached to one of the leading families in Amsterdam, but was it appropriate for him?

He did not feel attracted to Judith DaCosta. She was a pitiful woman, with no special charms. She carried her large body swathed in dark velvets, expecting sympathy and attention from everyone who crossed her way in the mansion. Yet when her sister-in-law Ruth DaCosta, or her brother Jeronimo DaCosta showed her any kindness, she rebuffed them. She proclaimed haughtily she had no need for their pity, that she was fine as she was.

She often sat downstairs in the living room, embroidering endless tulips and carnations with golden and purple thread on massive linen tablecloths for banquets that would never be staged in her honour. She rarely associated with other women except when there was a funeral. She seemed to take great pleasure in funerals. Whenever a Jew died, whether or not she had associated with the deceased when she or he was alive, she put on her best clothes and headed to the Ouderkerk cemetery in a funeral boat.

She made a great show of entering the funeral boat from the landing in front of their house and arranging herself regally on satin cushions. She was always treated courteously by the boat and barge operators. She tipped them well. It was rumored among the Gentile servant girls that she had enjoyed a secret dalliance with one of the boatmen before her marriage. Judith DaCosta dismissed such insinuations with annoyance and stated that the least she could do for those who earned their living by water was to tip them in memory of her beloved husband.

The servant girls denied her justifications maliciously. They said that her husband was not dead, since his body had never been recovered. "How is it possible," Samuel had heard the girls ask themselves in the kitchen, "that her husband is the only one missing from a crew which managed to swim to a nearby island? He must be hiding on an island, glad to be free of the surly giantess," they tittered. "Even a savage would make a kinder wife," commented the cook, who was the least talkative among them. How could Samuel bring himself to court such a woman? He reminded himself that despite his inexperience, he had attracted the affection of the two servant girls, Annetje and Jannetje, so perhaps he wasn't as hopeless with women as he believed. It could be that the servant girls liked him because he didn't demand much from them, never ordered them around, never asked them to bring him anything special from the kitchen. Perhaps they liked him because he was so different from the rest of the household, because he had once been a devout Catholic himself and did not begrudge them their time off for church and prayer.

He knew he was the forgiving kind. Perhaps his early years filled with prayer at the monastery, his later years at the seminary spent on a careful scrutiny of the sins of the world for which Jesus had died, his deep-felt urge to do what is right in the eyes of God, all this separated him from the average man. The girls and anyone else who had known poverty or loss or profound pain sensed this about him and happily tolerated his idiosyncracies.

"The DaCostas admitted you into their bosom and gave you a chance other new Jews would die for, and yet you notice only the kindness of Christians," chided the voice inside Samuel's head. "It's hard to comprehend their methods and motives," responded Samuel. "I don't understand, for example, whether they are liberal in their thinking or orthodox. Do they really trust me or am I still being watched? Do they really hope that I will remain with them?"

"In Rome, do as the Romans do," counselled the voice inside him.

Samuel rose from the bed, determined to try his luck with Judith DaCosta. Maybe it was possible to merge his world with their world.

Judith Da Costa was sitting alone in the living room in front of a vase of tulips she had strategically placed in the light streaming from the window. She was sketching with black charcoal on thick drawing paper. From the middle of the stairs, Samuel could see the designs she had already completed. They were all crooked. Samuel felt pity for her. His students were better draftsmen.

Unaware of Samuel's presence, Judith DaCosta carefully sketched another tulip. She had a variety of beautiful tulips in front of her: a Semper Augustus, Yellow and Red Leidens, and Jeronimo DaCosta's favorite, a Generalissimo, for whose bulbs he had bid vast amounts at the Amsterdam stock exchange. Samuel wondered why Judith DaCosta used black charcoal to depict a flower whose prime attraction was its variegated colors. In contrast to the sullen woman dressed in dark brown, the tulips blazed with sensual appeal. The flaming red stripes of the Semper Augustus, and the rich reds, yellows, and creams of the other flowers created a festive sight in that otherwise somber room.

Samuel descended from the stairs with every intention of flirting. But as soon as he took a step forward on the black and white tiled floor, he was overcome with the nauseating sensation that he was acting in a badly scripted play. The same frustration as when he tried to practice the steps to the courante overtook him and he felt dizzy. Trying desperately to maintain his composure, he approached the woman and greeted her.

"Good evening, Señora DaCosta," he said. "I see you're drawing."

"Yes," said Judith DaCosta coolly.

"I wonder why you have chosen to draw these merry tulips in black," he asked with feigned interest.

"I am not painting, Señor Salvador. I am only experimenting with new embroidery designs."

Whether it was the defensive tone of her voice, or her repellent gaze through narrowed eyes, Samuel felt dizzy again. "Let me see," he said, and made an unnecessarily wide arc with his arm as he tried to reach her sketch paper. Before he or Judith DaCosta could react, he had knocked the vase over.

The crash of the vase on the ceramic tiles brought the boys in from the kitchen, and Ruth DaCosta who was in the library yelled across the hallway to ask what had happened. Samuel bent over to pick up the flowers but when he saw the mangled tulips lying amidst the vase shards, he decided to sweep the mess instead. He was about to ask for a little brush and dustpan when his eyes met Judith DaCosta's glare. She would exact her revenge. There was no mistaking the look in her eye.

"Señor Salvador claimed that travellers were exempt from eating kosher meat," said Jacob DaCosta, his youngest student. "He also said that if he's invited to the house of a Gentile for dinner, and if he is the only Jew present, he will eat pork without hesitation."

Jacob's brother, Daniel DaCosta, said that when Samuel was describing life in Portugal and the customs of the Marranos there, he had joked that the poor souls believed that Yom Kippur was Dia Pura, "the Pure Day", and they accordingly cleaned themselves and their houses and fasted, assured that they would be duly cleansed by The Lord. "He told us he was disillusioned to discover that Yom Kippur did not cleanse the Jews, as he once thought."

At first, Isaac Nassi denied hearing Samuel make any improper declarations. However, upon further questioning by the rabbi in charge of conducting the inquiry, he admitted that he was surprised to hear Samuel compare the Jewish Talmud Torah to the Inquisition. "He said they have no right to act as censors, which they do when they ban publications whose contents do not suit their beliefs. He is also against the interdiction of exchanging books with Gentiles, your honour," said Isaac.

When questioned longer by the rabbi, Isaac remembered a comment Samuel had made when they were discussing the chronology of the world. "He questioned whether the world started at the time of Moses," said Isaac. "He told us that there was evidence that the Chinese people, who had raised a column for every passing year, had erected over ten thousand columns. So, he asked us, how the world could be only a little over five thousand years old."

The worst charge against Samuel was brought unwittingly by Joseph Prado. Joseph agreed that in class, Samuel had spent an inordinate amount of time describing Spain and Portugal and the Inquisition. When he saw the rabbi's eyes grow wide with interest, he tried to soften his remark by noting that they had repeatedly asked him to tell of his experiences there because he was such a good storyteller.

"Did he declare anything that would lead you to believe he

regretted his decision to embrace the religion of his forefathers?" asked the rabbi slyly.

"No, not at all. In fact, he criticized the Spanish government often."

"What did he say, for example?"

"He was critical of the Spanish government's insistence on the purity of blood which barred many New Christians from occupying positions of honor in the government."

"So he regrets he wasn't a Catholic of long standing..."

"He never said that," answered Joseph.

"But he did admit that he could not have held a high post in Spain because of his blood..."

"No he didn't," insisted Joseph.

"But he did not believe then that Jews were the Chosen People of God since he saw it as a disadvantage to have come from Jewish stock," argued the Rabbi.

"No, I mean yes, because he said that any law that discriminated against a person because of his heritage was a false law, requiring improvement."

"So he blasphemed by denying the Laws of Moses?" pressed the Rabbi.

Joseph, flustered, agreed. "I suppose so, your honour," he conceded.

Following the recommendation of the rabbi who had conducted the inquiry against Samuel, Samuel was excommunicated by the congregation Talmud Torah on a sunny fall morning. The regents of the synagogue read the edict of excommunication against Samuel as they stood in front of the holy ark at the Sabbath service. The service was well attended by the honorable members of the Portuguese Jewish community. All members of the Da-Costa family were present, and so was the printer and rabbi Menasseh ben Israel, who had welcomed Samuel to the bosom of the Jewish community a mere four years earlier.

Samuel listened to the charges brought against him with an impassive expression which revealed none of the bitterness he felt at those who curtailed free thought and free speech. While the rabbi who had conducted the inquiry detailed the heresies Samuel had committed against Judaism and declared him an ingrate who had not appreciated the efforts of the community which had strained its resources to integrate him when he had arrived penniless with a head full of confused ideas from a life spent among Catholic theologians, all Samuel could think of was the dream he had had about a year ago.

The swollen lips of his grammar teacher Senhor Torcato replaced the thin lips of the rabbi reading the charges and Samuel heard Senhor Torcato urge him, as he had once before in his dream, to unfurl his tongue from the protective sheath where he had stored it for the first forty years of his life. The face of the rabbi was now a blur, as were the faces of the regents who stood in front of the holy ark. Samuel was forty years old and he had freed his tongue from its hiding place. The velvet curtains concealing the ark were parted. The holy ark shone brilliantly, displaying its glorious ornaments.

Whether he would speak his mind by uttering words that were audible to the world, or by silently acknowledging his true thoughts, Samuel felt he would no longer be capable of self-censorship. "It is odd how the world bans you when you no longer ban yourself from yourself," the voice inside of him commented.

The charges were long and scandalous. Samuel, who had been praised as a good teacher, was now considered a threat to young Jewish minds. Samuel, who had once been considered an eligible bachelor was now considered an undesirable match for even the homeliest spinster or widow.

Samuel was duly banned from all of the Jewish community

activities for a period of six months. He would not be allowed to attend any services, seek employment or social relations with the members of the Congregation Talmud Torah, or be able to receive charity. If at the end of the temporary ban of six months he demonstrated proper repentance, the ban would be lifted. If he had not petitioned for a pardon and gave no reason to the elders of the synagogue that he would mend his ways, he would be excommunicated for good.

Samuel stood at the corner of the synagogue, unable and unbidden to respond. Jeronimo and Ruth DaCosta ignored him as they stood up from their seats and made their way slowly to the door. His students who had supplied the evidence against him bowed their heads as they passed in front of him. Only Judith DaCosta looked him in the eye, glowering. As she passed in front of him, she sputtered as if to spit at his feet. Samuel quickly examined his shoes. They had remained dry.

Samuel knew about the hostile behaviour of the congregation after similar sentences of excommunication. He had come as prepared as anyone can be for public rejection. He was fortunate that he had been spared extreme public humiliation. A few years earlier, the same congregation had thought nothing of ordering an accused man to lie prostrate at the door of the synagogue after the edict of excommunication had been declared, inviting those present to trample and kick him on their way out.

The rabbi Menasseh ben Israel lingered behind the crowd and approached Samuel. "In God's name, my son, ask for a pardon," he urged. "All this will be forgotten if you admit your faults. Your intellect is too precious, your knowledge of Latin impeccable. You may still regain your honour with us."

Samuel nodded although he was undecided as to what his response would be. Maybe all this was as it should be. Maybe he should leave Amsterdam, although he had no inkling how he would be able to finance his departure. "I'll come by your print shop to discuss my plans," he said quietly.

The rabbi drew back, agitated. "Oh, no, that will not do. Your presence in my premises may cause trouble for me. It is best if we meet someplace faraway from the common crowd. Perhaps if we meet on the outskirts of Amsterdam... at the cemetery, maybe."

"The ground has ears," said Samuel.

"What did you say, son?" asked the rabbi.

"As it was in Spain," said Samuel. "The ground has ears in Amsterdam."

The rabbi smiled uneasily. It was true that what he asked of Samuel now that he was excommunicated was no different than what the Marranos used to practice in Catholic lands where any conversation among them would be dangerous, and therefore best conducted in a secluded spot. "It's for the best, this way," he said. "For both of us," he added.

"Certainly, your honour," said Samuel.

When Samuel left the DaCosta residence for good that evening, he was allowed to take all his personal belongings and books. He packed his frayed copy of the Latin grammar text in his bag, but left the dance manual on the table beside his bed. The DaCostas were courteous to the end. Neither Jeronimo nor Ruth DaCosta spied on him as he was packing. They trusted that he would not make off with what was not rightfully his. In any case, he had exhibited a distaste for useless knickknacks when he asked that they be removed from his room when he first moved in. He did not appreciate objects of wealth enough to steal them. He had repeatedly amused the DaCostas and the servant girls when he observed a change in the silverware at mealtimes, confused that a shinier, more ornamental knife had been substituted for the one he had used the day before. He could not comprehend how a knife that had cut well could be supplanted by a duller one and still be called finer only because it was of purer silver.

Samuel left behind all the clothes that had been given to him by Jeronimo DaCosta: the satin house jacket which he was required to wear for the evening meals at the dining hall, the soft sheepskin slippers so that he would not make a sound at night to disturb the other sleepers in the household, the linen shirts with pleated cuffs, the velvet breeches. As he lay those clothes on his bed, one on top of the other in a sizeable heap, he felt curiously relieved as if he were shedding old skin with the costumes that had complemented his docile mask.

His students were not allowed to visit him in his room while he packed, but they politely lined up at the door to bid him goodbye. Ruth and Jeronimo DaCosta were stiffly formal. Judith DaCosta smiled haughtily, occasionally drawing in deep breaths as if she had exerted herself unnaturally before coming to the door. Annetje and Jannetje also stood by the door, quietly crying. Annetje lifted her apron to wipe her tears. Jannetje put her arm around Annetje to comfort her.

Samuel bowed courteously in front of each of his students and the servant girls as well as his employers. Jeronimo DaCosta extended his hand and Samuel automatically extended his, assuming they were about to shake hands. Instead, Jeronimo DaCosta quickly slipped a small envelope into Samuel's hand. "I suppose this will be all, then," he said and nodded, indicating that the farewells had been concluded. The women and children withdrew into the house and Jeronimo DaCosta quickly closed the door behind him.

Standing in the street, in front of the massive door, Samuel felt as if he had never stepped across that threshold, as if the mysteries of that patrician interior had never been revealed to him. He shrugged unselfconsciously, unaware that he was being watched through the window by Judith DaCosta. He had never actively pursued the mysteries of a wealthy life. Fate and chance had brought him through the DaCosta door, and now it was as if it had never opened for him.

Samuel walked a few paces then stopped. He had no idea where he would go next. Amsterdam was bustling with life at this hour. People were scurrying home for dinner, beggars extending their palms for the last alms of the day, children were being called indoors by harried grandmothers. In the canal across the street, boats had lined up to wait for the drawbridge to be lifted at the lock.

Samuel swung his bag down from his shoulder and set it on the cobblestones. He opened his right hand and lifted the crumpled envelope which had stuck to his sweaty palm. He opened the envelope. In it was a single ten guilder note and a scrap of paper. When Samuel unfolded the paper, he saw that it was a share of stock, bearing Jeronimo DaCosta's large signature, for a Generalissimo tulip bulb, to be redeemed at the stock exchange in the spring for a value of another ten guilders.

Samuel shook his head. The sight of the mangled Generalissimo tulip on the floor, amidst the broken glass, flashed before his eyes. Depending on the harvest and the market, the scrap of paper in his hands might be worth more or less in the spring. But spring was five months away. Until then he had only ten guilders. Receiving charity from the Jewish congregation was impossible. They had banned him. The Amsterdam burgomasters would not help him either. They respected the decision of the Jewish community to handle its own affairs and take care of its own members. Where was he to turn?

THREE

Your Giving is Our Living

SAMUEL SAT ON A ROCK by the Amstel river. In the distance the ruined roof of Kostverloren Castle emerged through the branches of the trees which had grown tall in the fertile soil around the castle's fortifications. Nearby, up the road, the large blades of a windmill paddled the cool air. The sky was unusually clear for a November afternoon, but a sharp northeasterly wind blew in gusts rustling the marsh grass.

Samuel huddled in his overcoat. The wind often got trapped in the marsh grass long after it had blown over the water. He watched with languid interest how the blades of grass lurched and swerved uneasily as if they had been imposed upon by a particularly disruptive guest who had trespassed upon them because they were so yielding and accommodating and unable to expel what was inimical to them.

The grass suffered the entry of the wind into its centre, while the blades of the windmill welcomed it and worked with it. As for the birds large and small, the sparrows and the sea gulls, they knew how to ride the wind, flapping their wings only when necessary, turning in circles above the river, alighting when the wind was weak, rising again when it gathered intensity.

Samuel was sitting just outside the city boundary of Amsterdam. A few paces away from where he sat, a stone column bearing the inscription, Terminus Proscriptionis, announced the limits of the city. The vaguely menacing copper ball and spike on top of the column were an additional reminder to birds, beasts, and exiled humans like Samuel that the ground in front of the post was the last place to rest before the independent judiciary powers of Amsterdam came into effect.

As he sat alone, watching the flat grey water, Samuel's ears grew accustomed to the rustle of the wind through the reeds and the occasional flap of a sea gull's wings. Soon, he felt his spine become as immobile and impervious as the plinth which marked the Amsterdam city limit. He was startled to hear a distinctly rhythmical scratching sound behind him. What creature could be making this insistent clawing, he wondered. He looked around, searching the ground for a burrowing animal, or a cat or rabbit that had wandered far from its homestead. He was so convinced that the sound came from an animal that he was shocked to notice a portly old man, dressed in several layers of coats standing behind him. When had this man arrived? How quietly he must have approached, like a seasoned hunter who knew not to draw attention to himself.

The man was holding a tablet of paper affixed to a piece of board in his left hand, and with his right hand, he made marks on the paper with a quill pen. He dipped his pen into his large coat pocket which Samuel surmised contained a bottle of ink, and withdrew it again to start scratching anew. When the man lifted his head, Samuel saw that he was squinting to see the skyline of the distant shore past Samuel's shoulder. The man swiftly returned his gaze to the paper. With the downward movement of his head, the wide brim of his hat fell over his eyes, covering them.

Samuel waited until the man's agitated scratching subsided before he greeted him.

"Good day, sir," he shouted across the wind.

"Good day to you, sir."

"Samuel Salvador," replied Samuel.

"Myself, old Rembrandt," answered the man in turn, breaking into a wide grin.

"The famous Rembrandt?" asked Samuel, incredulous.

"None other than himself."

"I hope I wasn't in your way?" asked Samuel.

"No, sir," replied Rembrandt. "I was drawing the shoreline. I hope I haven't disturbed your meditations."

"A respite from my thoughts is welcome, dear master," replied Samuel.

"All is well, then," said the old artist, "good day sir." Rembrandt tucked his block of paper under his arm and walked up the winding path toward Diemen, leaving Samuel to contemplate once again the slow and rhythmic paddling of the windmill blades through the air.

Samuel was not yet officially exiled, but rather in that purgatory period between being exiled from the Jewish community of Amsterdam and being exiled from Amsterdam itself by the burgomasters. If he found a way to earn his living outside the Jewish community, he could remain in Amsterdam as long as he wished, unless he became a public menace.

It was hard to avoid becoming a public menace. Without any financial help from the Jewish community, he had no one to turn to. He had no parents or relatives. Since he was not married, he could not count on the relatives of his wife. Since he had no children, he could not hope for the assistance and care given to many useless men by their children. He had no close friends. As a Jesuit he had counted on the institutions of Catholicism to support him. As a Jew he had relied on the goodwill of the Jewish community to provide him with jobs and money. Now, he was utterly alone.

In this he was different from the other Jews in Amsterdam, even the poor and uncultured ones that arrived from Polish and German lands, escaping ragtag from famines and massacres. All the other Jews, even when they arrived friendless or penniless, soon found others like themselves in Amsterdam, and organized among themselves to find lodging and food. Some turned to thieving and begging. Others tried to hire themselves out for day jobs in construction or for portering jobs at the harbour. Those who could tried to save enough money so that they could purchase pots and a small stove to set up a food stall or buy a lathe to sharpen knives on the street. They were miserable creatures, crude and brutish. But they were boisterous in their efforts to cling to the city, and they had invited Samuel into their midst.

When Samuel was dismissed from his job at the DaCosta household he had nowhere to go to spend the night. The fishmonger who had sold Samuel his dinner of fried herring stuck in half a loaf of bread that evening told him to go to the warehouse on Jodenbreestraat close to St. Anthony's Lock. There Samuel found about hundred or so men, thirty-odd women, and a few young children of both sexes in tattered clothes, making themselves comfortable among rags and old scraps of blankets, each in their own spot among the piles of hay and sawdust. Some had secured a measure of privacy by setting up makeshift screens or partitions from oddly sized boards.

Others were gathered at the centre of the warehouse where a large lantern shed light on the efforts of two old men and an old woman who were making pancakes which they sold for a stuiver each. Around the stove, men huddled together in a circle, warming themselves. At first, Samuel could not make out their features in the dark, because outside of the circle of light cast by the lantern, there was not much light in the warehouse, except for the few oil lamps burning weakly in corners where a couple of friends or a small family were gathered.

Samuel was taken aback by the precariousness of their existence. It was hard to distinguish the people from the heaps of rags. A sharp acrid smell of urine blended with the nauseating odors of unwashed bodies, musty clothes, and rotting fish. Although the air was chilly outside with a cold steady rain falling, Samuel was grateful for the drafts that came through the walls of the warehouse; at least this provided some badly needed air.

Saul, the fishmonger who had invited Samuel to the warehouse, was sitting among the men gathered around the stove. When he saw Samuel, he recognized him immediately. Samuel was surprised at this but he quickly remembered that his clothes set him apart from these men. He was dressed in clean clothes which didn't smell. It was his lack of smell that differentiated him he realized with horror, and also, the absence of patches on his garments. His clothes were new enough so that the outline of each item was distinguishable from the other. His pants looked like pants instead of old sacks, his jacket was a different colour than his coat, their lapels fit over each other evenly. On his feet he wore matching shoes with their straps intact instead of ill-fitting clogs.

Once again Samuel felt out of place. But Saul kindly welcomed him to the circle and introduced him as a famous scholar, a teacher who had taught one thing too many to his students. "They decided to send him to us, instead," he said sarcastically.

Saul's friends howled with laughter. "Come sit down, master," one yelled at him in broken Dutch, "make yourself warm before you retire to sleep."

"This is no place to catch up on lost sleep," joked a younger man with an enormous bulbous nose. His friends laughed again and the man sitting next to him slapped him on the shoulder jovially.

Samuel tried to fit into the spot they had cleared for him. It took enormous effort for him to sit so close to others. He wasn't used to being pressed on all sides by people. He realized he had never experienced this before, the proximity of other bodies, the blending and confusion of boundaries. Even at the orphanage when he was little boy, they all had their own seats during classes; and at the refectory, where they had sat on long pews, each had their own place to eat which was never changed from the day a boy entered the orphanage to the day he left.

At the seminary as well, he had been alone by choice and by discipline. Young Jesuits never touched each other. Whenever he and Alonzo Melami, his best friend, sat close to speak of their personal hopes, a Jesuit father had always separated them. They were promptly assigned chores in different parts of the seminary so that they wouldn't be able to meet again until dinner.

What was he to do among these people? He needed a place to stay, and he had no other place to go, but what could he talk to them about? Their squalor disgusted him. To his horror he realized he would soon look like them. Where would he go during the day? The thought of following them around for company to the ale-houses alarmed him. What would he do for food? He still had a few guilders to last him a few weeks if he were careful. What then? He did have the tulip stock from Senor DaCosta for the Generalissimo tulip. But it was probably worthless given how tulip prices fluctuated.

He was startled to hear a rattle close by, followed by strange chirping sounds. From the snickers of the men around him,

Samuel surmised that something was amiss, but he couldn't make out anything in the dark. A different fetid smell, an animal smell, was approaching him. Finally, he perceived a lean man standing upright with a crooked hat perched rakishly on his head. The man was holding onto a staff from which hung something like a lantern except that there was no light coming from it. Samuel was sure the strange screeching and chirping came from the lantern. The men around him laughed among themselves, amused by Samuel's bewildered looks.

When he focused his eyes on the lantern-shaped object dangling from the staff, he was appalled to see several rats with red beady eyes circling around what was a crude cage, not a lantern at all. Then he noticed the dried objects which had made the rattling sound. A wave of nausea swept over him. The rattle came from the desiccated pelts of dead rats rubbing against each other. The dead vermin had been tied together by their tails to a piece of rope that hung from a board at the bottom of the cage. They were so dry that they looked brittle. Their shriveled heads clicked when they bumped into each other.

The rat man cleared his throat before he saluted Samuel. "Welcome brother," he said. "Among us, everyone has a place, even these." He pointed at the restless rats in the cage above his head.

"Don't scare the teacher," retorted Saul, the fishmonger. "He has seen enough today."

Samuel smiled weakly in appreciation.

"Brother," said the rat man, "I've got the poison if you've got the rats."

"He has the best medicine in the city against the plague," yelled the young man with the bulbous nose. His friends guffawed again. At the far corner of the warehouse, away from the group of men, a baby wailed loudly.

"Go give the boy a rattle. It would surely please his mother," said the young man to the rat-poison man. His friend who seemed to enjoy everything that came out of his mouth poked him in the ribs.

After about an hour of sitting around, listening to such banter, and eating the half pancake which Saul had offered him, Samuel was shown a spot where he could curl up for the night. Finally alone, if one can be called alone in the midst of many men sneezing, snoring, and sighing in the darkness, and children wailing, Samuel prayed for help. In a drafty corner of the warehouse Samuel prayed to someone who oversaw all that was living, someone with power to guide him: God of Jews and Christians, angels and men, animals and vegetables.

Although it had been hours since Samuel lay down on his makeshift pallet of hay, which he had covered with the spare wool jacket and breeches he had packed into his sack when he left the DaCosta household, he believed he had not slept a wink. In fact, he had been sleeping a different sleep, one that was pierced by the howling wind outside his shelter and by the sounds of other bodies dreaming nearby, sighing and sucking on their dry tongues, turning over in vain seeking comfort on their hard beds.

Samuel opened his eyelids when he felt a purplish white light upon them. It was a familiar light, an urgent and vitalizing light which Samuel did not question. At the orphanage in Portugal where he had spent his childhood, he and the other orphans had been awakened by such a light at dawn as they lay on their narrow beds in neat rows. During those precious moments of sleep before the matins bell sounded, the orphans had been prodded by the milky grey light which streamed through the undulate pane of leaded glass in the only window of the dormitory.

Also, in a Jesuit outpost in northern Spain where he had

been sent once as a replacement for a priest who had suddenly fallen ill with catarrh and died, he had slept in a room above an old barn where a similar light had filtered through the skylight. He was still a student at the seminary then, young and hopeful, and had arrived with conviction at the desolate mountain village where the Basque flock attended his services at the chapel more for warmth than for consolation.

The purplish white light lit Samuel's face, then moved down his body. He was amazed to see himself awash in this bright light which touched no one else in the warehouse. Samuel turned to the wall to see if a crack had been rent there by the wind or if someone was holding a lantern over him. He had the eerie sensation that he had stepped into a religious painting made by any one of the itinerant painters who had generously adorned the small chapels in Spain with creamy luminous paint.

"Samuel," he heard someone whisper.

"Yes," he responded, propping himself up on his elbows.

"Samuel, it's me," said the voice. "You know me well."

"I do?" asked Samuel, incredulous.

"You do, shh, you do."

The light shifted a little to the side, and Samuel saw the thin long shape of a wise old man with bright blue eyes. The purple light massed around his shoulders, lending the appearance of a cloak, or even wings.

"I've been with you before," the man said. "But this is the first time you called for me."

"I did?"

"Yes, you called me by my name, before you fell asleep."

"Who are you?"

"Sealiah, the guardian of vegetables, fruits, grass, reeds, and other green things."

"I called you?"

"I was always with you, Samuel, from the beginning. You have traveled far, but so have I. I will help you."

"How?" asked Samuel, childlike. "Why?"

"Don't throw away the paper," Sealiah said.

"Which paper?"

"Tulips," answered Sealiah. "Tu-lips," he whispered again, and grew like a flower stretching toward the sun. Then he opened up like a bulb, offering enormous soft petals from its hard core. He disappeared after that, like a drop of dew pulled into the ether by the morning sun.

Samuel lay awake in the dark while everyone around him slept. The pain in his heart had disappeared. He was sure his heart had been touched by an angel, but he was puzzled by the mystery of this visitation. If Sealiah ruled over vegetables and fruits and grass as he had claimed, how could he cure hearts? Vegetables and fruits had no hearts. Their seeds and their centres were of the same matter as their outer layers. Their futures grew out of their seeds without the help of a heart which measures our time on earth. What was he to do with this mystery? How could he, whose pain came from the heart because it was so vulnerable and needy for other hearts to understand it, benefit from the counsel of an angel who ruled over heartless beings?

The angel had mentioned tulips. What secret lay in the realm of tulips? Samuel had never particulary liked tulips. They had no aroma. As a child, he had admired wilder, perfumed flowers, hardier blooms that prospered in the unruly gardens of the Iberian peninsula. Tulips with their reserved patrician blooms on their upright slim stems reminded him too much of the orderliness of Holland. He had never been inclined to linger in front of little gardens where wealthy burghers cultivated them. Neither was he able to comprehend the craze with which their bulbs were traded. He had lost his job at the DaCosta household after he had overturned a vase of tulips. As if to mock him further, they had paid him with tulip stock upon his dismissal. But if Sealiah were to help him, maybe that piece of paper would amount to something. Samuel instinctively reached into the breast pocket of his jacket where against the lining, he felt the little piece of paper. He had fallen asleep with that crumpled piece of paper placed over his heart.

Soon the sleepers in the warehouse began stirring. Some rose from their makeshift beds, stretching their limbs, shaking the numbness off their hands and feet, turning their necks left and right to ease the pain of convoluted postures unwittingly kept during the night. Others remained on the floor, gazing at the rafters with languid eyes, searching for their reason to rise. Babies wailed and were quickly brought to their mothers' breasts. Children who coughed the dry hacking cough of poverty were not heeded. A warm cup of tea would be found later, after several hours of collecting alms.

Samuel got up and wore his coat over the clothes he had slept in. Around him others were doing the same, layering themselves for the damp Amsterdam day ahead. There was a smoky, stuffy warmth inside the warehouse which, compared to the unknown perils of the day, felt safe. But it was no place to remain. Only those that were to ill to beg or to sell their salves, poisons, and charms, or too old to walk, would stay behind with the nursing mothers.

Saul advised Samuel to leave his sack of clothes on the spot where he had slept to assure his place for the following night. "Take your valuables along with you, though," he warned. "Don't worry about the rags," he added with a bitter smile. "We all find plenty of those."

Samuel secreted his sack of clothes under a mound of hay where he had rested his head during the night. Then he propped a plank on its side to shield his bed so that it would not be muddied and soiled by the comings and goings of the people who would pass that way to reach the door.

As he was preparing to leave, he heard a heavy rapping on the floorboards as if someone was beating grains with a large pestle. He turned and came face to face with Captain One-Leg, the notorious schemer of Amsterdam who had become a legend in his lifetime. Captain One-Leg's name was sung by bards in smoky taverns where women of ill-repute routinely robbed inebriated sailors of their money pouches. His gait was imitated by nannies of patrician children who threatened their charges with abduction by Captain One-Leg unless they stopped mis-behaving. Although he was not a Polish or German Jew like the residents of the warehouse, Captain One-Leg apparently sought his friends here, away from his co-religionists, the Anabaptists he had not hesitated to cheat. Here were people who shared his destiny; here were wayfarers condemned to travelling long distances every day precisely because they, too, were crippled by poverty and uprooted in spirit.

Captain One-Leg hailed a friend by raising his cane and pointing its tip toward his friend's head. His friend broke into a wide grin and waved back with both arms, motioning Captain One-Leg to wait a while. Samuel saw with amusement that Captain One-Leg's friend was the young man with the bulbous nose who had made all the wisecracks when they were huddled around the pancake stove. The young man had chosen a fine master to apprentice to. He would go further than all the other quacksalvers and beggars.

As the young man walked past Samuel toward the door, he

asked if Samuel wanted to join them for a glass of warm ale. Samuel declined the invitation, but thanked him nevertheless. He watched the two men leave the warehouse and make their way along the canal toward Houtgracht, Captain One-Leg's wooden peg reverberating dully on the cobblestones.

One Saturday in late November several weeks after he had moved into the warehouse on Jodenbreestraat, Samuel felt the urge to walk toward the Portuguese synagogue where he had been condemned for speaking his mind. Like a criminal drawn irresistibly to the scene of his crime—like an exile who yearns for the land he has been expelled from—Samuel wanted to see the synagogue where the Sephardic notables who had drawn him into their midst as soon as he had arrived in the city, and he, himself, had congregated every Sabbath.

He stood on the bridge across from the synagogue. At this early hour of the morning, the streets were still deserted. The canals, however, were already busy with boats and barges delivering bread, vegetables and fruit, salted herring, and peat to the Saturday market. Samuel leaned over the railing and stared at the canal. The dark water of the canal drew him in like a well, but this was a well which extended radially.

The canals of Amsterdam were arteries which nourished the life that had been built above water. Samuel enjoyed this paradox of earth above water, solidity over fluidity that defined Amsterdam. In Spain and Portugal the earth had been dry, as dry as old dogmas, dusty with time, but in Amsterdam, which was often shrouded in fog, frequently wet with rain, the earth was only a compromise between water below and water above.

It was hard for Samuel to hold onto a solid thought when the clothes on his back always felt damp against his skin. His convictions became as soggy as the wood of the pylons on which the city stood. His mind had become flexible here, but he felt he had also absorbed too much doubt, too much indecision, and was weighted down like an amphibian which is always drawn to water however high it attempts to leap. A frog will never grow wings however hard he tries.

From the bridge, Samuel could observe the activity inside the Lazaretto. Through the kitchen window, which faced the canal, he could see the Calvinist caretakers who were preparing soup for their wards before dismissing them to the streets for the day. Once he had envied those poor beggars and lepers for the companionship they enjoyed among themselves. Once his solitude in the small room across the Lazaretto had been tinged with a sadness that had made the memories of his orphaned youth seem all the more clear—as a chilly breeze will sharpen the outlines of trees and houses on a winter night. He had been envious of the faint light of oil lamps in the dormitory of the Lazaretto, the orange glow of the beggars' pipes, the smoky warmth of their breaths intermingling with each other.

Now that he was alone once again, although in the company of others in that stinky warehouse, he no longer envied such proximity. It was meaningless. A yearning heart is never warmed by the presence of other hearts. Perhaps that was the message of the angel Sealiah. Perhaps his search for an ideal place to live, a family of blood kin, or the fellowship of like minds was all in vain. Perhaps he had never truly listened to his heart's message. He had been too busy deciphering the meaning of abstruse passages in too many books, too preoccupied with the interpretation and translation of slippery words from one language to another. In the meantime, he had wandered away from his own soul.

What did he want from the world and the life that was given to him? He was blessed with a fine constitution. All the shifts in his fortune had not marred him physically. His gait was still strong and even, his breath was not labored even when he walked for hours in the driving rain. He could still climb up the narrow stairs of tall Amsterdam buildings without stopping at landings to catch his breath. Other men his age, burdened with a wife and children, weighted by the worries of business if they were well to do, or worn down by labour if they were poor, often had less vitality than him. The thought that he was a better survivor than most men his age calmed him. He could still travel on if he wished. There was still hope for him to change his life.

The street was becoming more crowded. Among a group of men heading toward the synagogue, he noticed a few patrician Jews wearing large brimmed hats ornamented with exotic plumes. The stocky man with the short black velvet cape was Dr. Bueno, a famous surgeon, engaged in a passionate discussion with the merchant Leo Duarte, who traded in precious stones. When Señor Duarte waved his hand in the air as if to dismiss a suggestion made by Dr. Bueno, the squarely cut blue gem at the centre of the ring he wore on his little finger glistened in the light.

Behind them, Samuel observed the DaCosta family descending from a fancy carriage. He watched Judith DaCosta gather her skirts before she took a step down. She could barely bend her bonneted head to heed her step. The large stiff white collar around her neck inhibited all movement. Señor DaCosta, who had stepped down first, lent his sister a hand. A gentleman at all times, he skilfully hid his resentment towards the sister who demanded his care without giving any in return. DaCosta's sons, his former pupils, leapt down from the carriage, followed by their mother who descended without any help since her husband was still busy with his sister who was leaning on his arm.

Although they were close enough to recognize him, they

seemed leagues away, in another country. When they gazed in his direction, Samuel felt anxious that they would recognize him. He reminded himself, however, that his weeks at the warehouse had altered his looks. He had become indistinguishable from the other wretches who populated the streets of Amsterdam. He was wearing the old cap Saul had given him, and his green coat was already torn in places. He had taken to stepping on the back of his shoes, wearing them like clogs to ease the pain of his swollen feet. The DaCostas would not be able to identify him.

He wished he could go into the synagogue with them, be accepted once again, and made welcome, but the desire passed as quickly as it had appeared. He smiled wanly at the thought that the Ashkenazi synagogue would not close its doors to him because he was indistinguishable from the German and Polish folk who begged, traded in rags, and operated the street stalls along the canals.

He sauntered toward the Ashkenazi synagogue on the other side of the canal. The ambiance changed immediately. Although the Ashkenazim had arrived from nearby countries in Eastern Europe, they looked more like the original Jews of the Bible, unchanged by thousands of years of history. They were also humbler, aware of their difference, and cognizant of their faint chances for advancement into the cosmopolitan circles of Amsterdam. Most of them were shabbily dressed. Samuel recognized the rat-poison man, without his odious rat cage, and his young friend with the bulbous nose. They greeted him, but did not stop to make small talk. He was surprised to see a female singer from a tavern at the fish market where he had spent a few evenings nursing a tankard of jenever in a dark corner, enter the synagogue. He hadn't realized she was a Jewess.

Samuel sat on a stone slab in front of the synagogue. Around him old men were talking in pairs, whispering gossip and platitudes into each other's ears. What news were they sharing that was so interesting? Perhaps they were discussing the recent news from the New World that the Sambatyon river had been conclusively located there.

Samuel sat with his back turned to the street, his left hand cupping his chin, his shoulders rounded. The rabbi's assistant came out to announce that they needed a few more men to complete a minyan. Samuel didn't budge. A couple of men quickly went in. The whispers subsided. Samuel was unable to decide whether he should go in. Soon, he heard the same scratching sound he had heard on the banks of the Amstel river. This time he knew where it was coming from. He turned around and saw the artist Rembrandt, finishing a drawing of him and the other men in front of the synagogue. He smiled. He got up to look at the drawing. It was a true likeness of him. The slope of his shoulders, his cap squashed flat on his head like an Oriental headdress, his left hand with the fingers curled like a fist under his chin, all had been captured by the artist.

Rembrandt asked him if he intended to go in.

"I don't think so," answered Samuel.

"That's what I thought," said Rembrandt.

"How could you tell?" asked Samuel, surprised.

"Your shoulders didn't move when the rabbi's helper announced he needed more men," answered Rembrandt.

"You noticed that?"

"I had to. I was drawing them," said Rembrandt. "Would you like to come to my house for some tea, instead?

Samuel was puzzled. Why would a well-known artist offer to take him home? It did not occur to him that Rembrandt could also be curious about him, that he might consider using him as a model.

FOUR

Rembrandt's Model

REMBRANDT AND HIS FUTURE MODEL ambled along the canals toward Rozengracht. With Rembrandt Samuel saw Amsterdam as he had never seen it before. The city seemed to speak to him through its shapes and textures, its gradations of colour and light, density and emptiness. He wondered what Rembrandt did to bring about this magical effect. Perhaps it was the leisurely way he walked, pausing in the midst of a sentence to angle his head to observe the shadow of a low-lying cloud on the façade of a gabled house, or the way he smiled ever so slightly when a beggar with a particularly theatrical costume crossed their path.

Samuel had never observed objects or people like this. His ears had always been attentive to languages, and written texts had certainly fascinated him. Nature, because it is God-given, and not man-made, had also demanded his attention. Because he could rest his mind in nature and take refuge in its simplicity, he had observed it. But, he had never paid much attention to the qualities of man-made things—their shapes, colour, size, and weight. Things had held his interest only when they were unique in the world, when the word describing them in one language was not translatable into another.

A door, for example, had always been a door for him whether it barred the entrance to a church or a synagogue, a hospital or a school. Perhaps because he had never known the comfort that the sight of a particular door could bring, the door of one's own house inside which a loving mother awaited him for example, all doors were exchangeable for him. What mattered to him was that a door performed its function, barring the outside from the interior, that it locked well. If it had a peculiarity, such as a crooked latch, or a keyhole that required the insertion of a key at an angle for it to open, well, he remembered that as well. But the colour of a door, the grain of the wood, the ornamental design around the border of a latch, these had been inconsequential to him. These little details of the world were but temporary and frivolous joys when there was so much to ponder and grasp in print.

As Samuel walked alongside Rembrandt, the world appeared to him in many more colors than the predictable contrast of black type against white paper. The sky that had been grey seemed to be composed of several hues of blue, green, and white. The dark blue canal water reflected the shadows of the bridges in rusty, reddish hues. Faces he would not have paid attention to before, those of the native Dutch Amsterdammers, sprang to life.

For the first time Samuel detected a resemblance to his own face in their faces. For so long, he had assumed that his face was that of a foreigner, hopelessly unmatched in this northern city where straight golden hair and light eyes were more common than the dark curls, deep brown eyes, and the aquiline nose of his Sephardic heritage. He had walked the streets of Amsterdam with a lonely anxious heart, his eyes searching for other Jews, hoping to find familiarity in the faces of his brethren around the

Jewish establishments.

Next to the artist Samuel felt the surge of vitality of a homecoming, and home was the street teeming with vendors, beggars, merchants, housewives, children, nannies, dogs and cats. Home was this street and any other street in the world; family was the boy with golden curls chasing a hoop beside the canal and his chubby sister running after her brother, skirts held up at her sides. Family was this artist bringing him home, the beggars he would share his night with at the warehouse, and Alonzo, wherever he was. The wide sky would shield them all.

Near Rozengracht the character of the houses changed, they were further apart from each other, but also older with many of them needing a fresh coat of paint. The residents were poorer and coarser, but friendlier. The old artist now lived in this section of the city. Rembrandt made Samuel welcome in the small but pleasant living room which was also the kitchen. Although the room was neat and orderly, in all its corners and shelves were the accoutrements of an artist: bottles and jars of various sizes for storing and mixing pigments, reeds and brushes standing upright in a large earthenware jug, boards of various sizes, and several empty frames stacked together in a corner.

Samuel sat by the large oak table while Rembrandt bustled to prepare tea. First, he put water to boil in a fire-blackened kettle on the stove in the centre of the room. Then he absent-mindedly opened and closed several cupboards searching for teacups and sugar. When he found them, he searched for the tea. He kept asking himself aloud where he might have put the tea. "Ceylon tea, Ceylon tea," he repeated, as if the incantation would help materialize the tea. He finally found it where he had left it, on the floor beneath the wash basin, in a blue glass jar.

When the water finally boiled, Rembrandt poured the water into a three-legged pewter urn standing on the table, and added a measure of Ceylon tea. He set out two blue ceramic tea cups, surprisingly delicate and expensive looking, considering the humble state of the house and the furniture. As the tea steeped in the large urn between them, Rembrandt quietly observed Samuel who was taking in the details of his surroundings.

From where he sat Samuel could see the backyard through the window. There was a narrow waterway at the end of the backyard where a small boat was moored to the low wrought-iron fence at the edge of the water. Samuel wondered if Rembrandt ever used the boat to reach the main canal.

Samuel became a frequent visitor at the Rembrandt house, modeling for Rembrandt as he drew sketches inspired by his favorite stories from the Old Testament. Quite rapidly, Rembrandt and Samuel developed a friendship far more intimate than what would be expected between an artist and his model. Although they shared their stories, with Samuel recounting his life in the Jesuit seminary and Rembrandt describing his old projects, discussing what he would do differently with what he knew now, and planning his future projects; it was their silences which suited each other best.

By nature and training Samuel was a good listener. Especially at this point in his life he liked to listen, for it was a respite from the hectic despair of the noisy warehouse where he continued to spend his nights. Dressed in the layers of vests, coats, and capes which Rembrandt asked him to wear, Samuel felt warm and protected in this new employment that demanded little from him, only that he sit patiently, like a prop in a theatre, and listen without nodding.

In Samuel's physique and profile, Rembrandt perceived an immense range of possibilities. In some sketches which were inspired by the Old Testament, Samuel became a Jewish hero; Mordecai on a horse triumphantly parading in the streets in front of King Ahaseurus and Queen Esther. In another sketch Samuel modeled for Tobias, the son of Tobit who returned home with the archangel Raphael and cured his father's blindness with the entrails of a fish. Rembrandt liked Samuel's well-defined profile and drew it often, sometimes adding a long beard, as in his sketch of the four dervishes, to accentuate his sharp nose.

By dressing him in one of the robes in his studio and wrapping a turban around his head, Rembrandt transformed Samuel into a dervish sitting on the floor with his knees raised, his arms comfortably resting on his knees, his hands invisibly joined inside the wide sleeves of his caftan. The three other dervishes were holding tea cups in their hands; arguing, no doubt, about a point of faith such as whether fasting was obligatory for travelers during the month of Ramadan. Meanwhile, the dervish who was Samuel listened to them intently, his own tea cup untouched on the tray in front of him.

In other drawings, Rembrandt represented Samuel as a Roman soldier, a face among the crowd listening to Christ deliver his sermon in a cave, or as St. Francis praying at the foot of a giant tree. Rembrandt borrowed Samuel's face to depict a beggar, a dwarf, a child, an alchemist, a sculptor, a goldweigher's assistant, a man listening to Joseph recount his dreams, an angel being entertained by Abraham, and even a lion smiling congenially at Daniel who was standing undaunted in the beast's den.

So intimate did Samuel's face become for Rembrandt that he could draw it from memory. He even dreamed of Samuel's face. Sometimes he woke up thinking he had known Samuel before, during his childhood in Leyden. Samuel's face blended with the faces of his classmates at the Latin school. Rembrandt would think of a sunny fall day he had skipped class with his friends, competing to see who could cross a canal more times on stilts without falling into the water, and Samuel's face would appear across the canal, announcing his victory, daring Rembrandt to match his record.

Sometimes Rembrandt thought that he had shared a pew with Samuel at the Latin school and that Samuel was the trusted friend who had quietly whispered the correct pronunciation of a word he stumbled on while being quizzed by their teacher. In his dreams Samuel never snickered at him like some of his classmates, who had ridiculed his ambitions of becoming a famous painter and marrying into a wealthy family.

What worried Rembrandt most was how Samuel's face sometimes took over his beloved wife Hendrickje's face in his dreams. He would be in a warm, reassuring dream, embracing Hendrickje and he would relax, forgetting that Hendrickje had been long dead. He would begin to feel the vitality of his younger years in his muscles, and the urge to tell all his debtors to wait a while longer until he sold another painting so that he could pay them off and get rid of them for good, or he would be in his studio in Breestraat, demonstrating drawing techniques to twenty eager students who were paying him well to hear him criticize their work, and there would be Samuel, with his thin long nose, his head slightly bent as always, smiling. Then, Samuel would be in his arms instead of Hendrickje. Sometimes Samuel rested his head on his chest. There was Samuel breathing deeply like a happy child at his father's bosom; there was Samuel unaware of the hold he had on the artist but sure that it was meant to last, smiling like a baby for he felt no need to question such attachments.

Rembrandt did not share these dreams with Samuel, but he became increasingly puzzled by the hold his model had on his psyche. He thought back to the first time he had brought Samuel home several months ago, after he had drawn the Jews in front of the synagogue. He went back to his portfolio of sketches and withdrew that sketch. He had drawn seven other faces, but

Samuel's was not among them. He had intuitively known to hide that face which had the power to insinuate itself into his dreams and to affix itself to bodies of varying sizes and divergent personalities. It was a face at home in vastly different historical epochs; it could calmly witness the birth of major religions.

Rembrandt scrutinized his other sketches until he found the one he had drawn of a bend in the Amstel River near Kostverloren Castle. He remembered the day he had drawn it, a windy day when colors and outlines had appeared especially sharp because of the wind. Huddled at the edge of the water had been Samuel, staring at the play of the wind in the clump of reeds ahead of him. Rembrandt had not even attempted to include him in the drawing. Often he made sketches of bodies and faces in the corner of a sheet on which he had sketched a landscape. By turning the sheet of paper around he would gain extra drawing space in the white empty spaces, and experiment with a different technique, or examine the various shading effects of a new ink, but he had done nothing of the sort the first time he had seen Samuel. He had known to avoid him.

Anxiously he examined the many faces of Samuel in his drawings. As long as he had changed the face, added a hat that was one of his own props, shaded in a beard that Samuel would not consider growing on his own face, or exaggerated the curve of his nose, Samuel's face belonged to him, the artist. Rembrandt laid aside the sketches where he had depicted Samuel more or less as he looked in real life. In those drawings, perhaps because he had placed Samuel as an insignificant character in a crowd, or as a face peering toward the centre of light from its dark corner, he had not bothered to change his face.

In a chiaroscuro, light draws the eye to itself; what remains in darkness is exalted because of the contrast. Simple, unadorned forms worked best in the dark corners of a sketch, but there lay the danger as well, for dark corners became more powerful, the longer a viewer gazed at a picture. The eye, curious about the periphery away from the centre of light, gathered information by way of guessing and imagining more than by observing. Thus, the mind became excited. Hungry for play as it always is, the mind remembered the details of the dark areas better, making whatever was there more potent.

This is how Samuel had gained power over Rembrandt, in the dark corners where the artist had placed him as he was in real life. Rembrandt sighed with relief. Now, he knew what to do. He would obscure the face even more where it appeared in the dark corners. As for the sketches where the face had been altered, he would alter them more. He would keep Samuel as a friend, but remove him from his dreams. A model had no business taking over the mind of an artist. He would ask Samuel to continue posing for him in the studio, for he enjoyed conversing with him, but he would not allow Samuel's face to take over his art.

Samuel, unaware of the effect he had on Rembrandt, did as he was bid and sat the poses the artist requested. The temporary ban which had exiled him from the Sephardic synagogue was nearing its end. He wondered if he should ask for a pardon, and beg his way in, or proudly stick to his own views, and refrain from repenting. Samuel asked these questions aloud as he sat with his back to Rembrandt who insisted that he wanted to capture the contours of his shoulder, not his face.

"Your face is etched into my mind, Samuel," Rembrandt stated with no trace of irony, but "the shoulders need attention."

Samuel sat hunched on a chest facing the stove in the centre of the studio. Rembrandt sketched the wooden chest as a stone seat flanking the entrance to the synagogue. Later, he had Samuel wear a long cloak and asked him to lean on a staff, and he sketched the folds of his cloak as it fell away from his body. These drawings were all part of the composition Rembrandt had decided to develop for an etching that would be called "The Jews in the Synagogue."

"Should I try and go back in?" Samuel asked.

"Depends what you want from your future," Rembrandt answered, matter-of-factly.

"If you want to return to your previous employment as a teacher, I would strongly urge you to seek their pardon and demonstrate that you have repented."

"Would they believe me?" Samuel wondered. "I haven't proved to them that I'm any different from the man they rejected. I have certainly lived among Jews in the warehouse, but those wretches are not the kind of Jews that the Sephardic notables would approve of. They might even consider me tainted in some way."

"Why?" asked Rembrandt.

"Because I have known poverty and endured it like a Christian who has sworn off material gain instead of appealing to the synagogue for help and mercy. Coming here to visit you," he added, "made it possible. But they don't know this, of course. I didn't return to them asking for pardon. I didn't ask my former employers to intercede on my behalf. I didn't make myself visible at the door of the synagogue."

"They must be wondering what happened to you, then," answered Rembrandt calmly. "People in power are always angry when those they believe inferior to them do not crumble under their might. Don't be shocked if they're angrier than when they first banned you."

"Sometimes banishment is what the soul needs to grow. I thought I was able to maintain a reflective solitude, but I wasn't.

Because I still wanted to fit in with them and because I thought I could find my family among them, I suffered."

"Those are noble and just desires," answered Rembrandt.

"But they are dependant on others for fulfillment," interjected Samuel. "Your life, on the other hand is your own because you are a painter. You are your own master."

"My creditors didn't share your assessment of my life," said Rembrandt, smiling bitterly. "If they had, I wouldn't be living here now."

"Then we wouldn't have met, either," responded Samuel.

"Why do you say that? I was surrounded by Jewish neighbors there."

"Precisely my point. You were surrounded by the very people who banished me from their midst."

"I would have drawn you, anyway."

"But you wouldn't have brought me home."

"That may be true, and may not be. Artists always bring home unlikely guests."

"On the other hand I might not have followed you home. You belonged to the world that I had so much trouble living in."

"Ah, that is also a possibility, of course," said Rembrandt. "You might not have desired my companionship. So, you see, you are your own master because, ultimately, you make your own decisions."

"That is not what I meant at all," responded Samuel abruptly.

"I know what you meant. I certainly know what you meant. Being a painter allows me to dictate my own life, but that does not mean I don't have a master."

"Who is your master, then?" asked Samuel.

"My talent. All these years I have been the servant of my talent."

"And I have sought knowledge—or it sought me. For

knowledge came to me without my asking for it. And I assumed that others would want what I know."

"They don't?"

"No, they don't. And maybe I persisted too long in places where there was nothing new to learn."

"Why, Samuel, you have mastered languages and religions. You have traveled and lived among the Jews and the Christians. You have studied both the Old and the New Testament. You speak Latin, Spanish, Portuguese, and Dutch. And now you probably speak Polish, after living at the warehouse."

"All words," Samuel said wearily. "They are all words, and none can pry open the seal on my heart."

"Ah, that," said Rembrandt.

Samuel looked at the aged artist who had put his pen down and grown still. "Do you possess the key to the heart?"

"For that you will have to ask yourself."

"I have been asking myself, and have heard nothing in response."

"A voice? A small voice where there is no one, a shaft of light where there is no lantern? Haven't you ever felt a chill where there was no draft?"

"That's the answer?"

"Perhaps," said Rembrandt.

At first Rembrandt had drawn Samuel's face because he liked his profile. When his face intervened in his dreams Rembrandt asked Samuel to turn his back so that he could master the contours of his shoulders, the line and volume of the muscles on his torso and limbs. When he could draw Samuel's body effortlessly under the folds of Roman togas, Persian kaftans, and Polish cavalry uniforms; when he could hint at the weight of his arms concealed in the loose sleeves of an Oriental robe, or sketch them bare in a jerkin, enwrap his hands in calf skin gloves owned by a patrician, insert his feet into Greek sandals or Medieval shoes, Rembrandt felt he knew Samuel well enough to ask him to feign emotions which he could then draw.

For all his serious and gloomy appearance, Samuel could smile. Although his smile reflected a sardonic bent, it was pleasant enough and came readily. His eyes became quizzical easily, his lips quickly curled upward at the thought of something comical. Laughter, too, he could produce with childlike glee. It was enough for him to think back to the orphanage in Portugal and the innocent tricks he and his friends played during recess period on the corpulent monk who was barely a few years older than his charges.

Laughter was also available to him when he thought of his students at the DaCosta household, the DaCosta brothers Daniel and Jacob, and their cousins, Joseph and Isaac. He had enjoyed teaching them in the comfort of that stately mansion with the high ceilinged rooms and marble tiled floors. His stories about the life on the Iberian peninsula had fired the boys' imaginations, and together they had concocted many fanciful tales about their return to Spain, where they would travel disguised as jugglers and acrobats who sought shelter in the Jesuit monasteries which Samuel had lived in or visited in his youth.

An expression of fright was harder to simulate. Samuel opened his eyes wide and tightened his jaws, but it was too theatrical for Rembrandt, who wished to capture everyday emotions in his art.

"The model has to look natural," he commented. "It is the artist's prerogative to make what is commonplace appear supernatural."

Samuel was unsure how to find the experience of fear in the depths of his soul. Although many frightful things had happened to him, he had moved from one event to the next with the equanimity of a man who has learned early in life to never take affection or shelter for granted. Affection and protection would come, but never in the expected ways. So what was the use of fear when life would provide sustenance in one form or another, in one country or another, under the rule of a king or queen, priest or rabbi?

"I can't do it," concluded Samuel. "Even my most frightening nightmares aren't horrific enough for me to give you what you want."

"Perhaps I should find another model, then," responded Rembrandt. "A simple man straight off the street with none of your learning." Eyes twinkling with amusement, Rembrandt then related a story that a friend of his, another painter, had told him.

"The painter in question was then living in Vienna. He wanted to paint a picture of the denial of Saint Peter and thought that he could find himself a suitable model among the countless beggars and vagabonds in the city, so he went to the marketplace. There, he persuaded a beggar, using the promise of a good payment— enough to feed a man for a whole week. The beggar followed the painter to the studio, but as soon as he saw the various props, swords, cloaks, masks and plaster busts, and especially, the skulls the artist used for his Vanitas paintings, he thought he was in the house of Satan and that he had been tricked by Death himself. He fell on his knees, begging for mercy, and for time to live longer. He confessed all his sins, all the small thefts and the adultery he had committed with his sister-in-law. He promised never to err again if he would be allowed to leave. When the painter offered him money to calm him and persuade him to stay, the man became more terrified. He was certain that Satan was bargaining with him to sell his soul, so he started crying and wailing."

"The painter, meanwhile, decided that the best course was

to let the terrified man wail as long as possible. He painted him in that state, with bulging eyes and outstretched hands pleading for mercy. He claimed that this was the most natural expression of fear he had observed on a model!"

"Even on the first day I followed you home I wasn't scared," Samuel said, between guffaws. "I'm used to props. The Catholic church is full of them. The synagogue is not lacking in them either. I was taught how to use props to incite fear and reverence in the commoners. So that's not a way to scare me, not at all."

It occurred to Samuel that for all his interest in theatrical costumes and props, Rembrandt used no organic props in his studio. "Why don't you ever sketch flowers?" he asked Rembrandt. "Surely, flowers bloomed in biblical times. You say you don't like tulips, so what about carnations or wild flowers? Why don't you ever bring them into the studio to sketch them?"

"I sketch flowers in nature," replied Rembrandt, "where they belong. Dressing up models doesn't involve uprooting them. Besides," he added, "live props are too expensive. They don't last long, either."

"Maybe not now, but there was a time you could have afforded to buy the most expensive tulip."

"Let me tell you another story then, one that happened when I was still living on Jodenbreestraat. Remember how fashionable it was to paint tulips for a while? Every Dutch painter painted them. Some went further and began cultivating them in their gardens. Their interest in cultivation led to an interest in tulip stocks, and soon, every artist with loose change was betting on the stock market."

"Anyway, this fellow, Cornelis—we used to call him 'Little Crab,' because of the shape of his hands, they were curiously large and malformed like crab claws. Cornelis had bought a very expensive tulip bulb which he hoped to resell the next day. He brought it home and laid it on a shelf in his kitchen. It so happened that he had visitors that evening, several other painters, and a man he often hired as a model. After they finished a bottle of jenever, Little Crab stepped out of the room to bring back another bottle. At that point the model, who often ate at Little Crab's house, saw the tulip bulb on the shelf. Thinking it was an onion, he ate it along with the half loaf of bread he found there. He didn't like the taste though, so when Little Crab returned, he complained that the only onion he could find in the place was rotten."

"You can imagine Cornelis' terror when he realized what had happened to his precious investment. Eaten by his own model, never to be recovered, except as excrement! Little Crab never recovered from the financial loss. He drank himself to death within a few years."

"I would know the difference between a tulip and an onion bulb," replied Samuel, "but you're right, why take a chance."

"I have painted lemons, though," added Rembrandt as an afterthought. "No one I know would be tempted to eat one."

"Except me," said Samuel. "You're lucky you have none here now, because I might have been tempted to eat a lemon. I grew up where lemons come from."

"You're right, I forgot about that. Even then, I've never painted ordinary lemons, but etrogs. You would not touch an etrog."

"The same etrogs that the synagogue pays so much money every year to purchase?"

"The very same etrogs."

"They look different from a lemon. When I first saw one I thought it was a diseased lemon. A cross between a quince and a lemon, that's what I thought it was."

"They are hard to find, but they keep well, and my Jewish

patrons have always approved of an etrog as a prop."

"Where did you get them anyway? From the synagogue?"

"I know the men who trade in them," replied Rembrandt. "Agents for the Corfiote Jews who cultivate them. In fact, they are due for a visit in the next few weeks. They always come a good six months before Sukkoth to take orders."

Days and weeks passed like this in Rembrandt's studio. The deadline on Samuel's ban came and went. Samuel considered asking for pardon from the elders of the synagogue, but decided against it. He had spent enough time with Rembrandt to learn that if you allow people the right to judge you, judge they will, and often. If he were welcomed back now they'd be threatening to cast him out again within the year. He had no desire to marry one of the daughters of the community, no wish to put on airs and mouth social niceties. He couldn't imagine being silent, either, as he had been when opinions he disagreed with were bandied about with insolence and downright ignorance. He admitted to himself that he had gained much spiritual good from his studies as a Catholic, and he wasn't about to dismiss his personal preference for loving and forgiving your enemy over arguing endlessly about how and when you were wronged so that you could secure a just retribution.

If one religion was the religion of the father, the other was the religion of the son. He had been born into the religion of the father, raised in the religion of the son, and had gone home to seek the father only to discover that the father was a man he could not live with. In essence the father and son were no different; both maintained their hold on their people by accusing the other. The two camps were locked in a never-ending battle and the best they could manage, in a place like Amsterdam, was a tournament of mutual distrust accompanied by minimal exchange on the most cordial of terms which left no hope for true understanding.

If Samuel could have his way, he would leave both the father and the son behind and find himself a religion of friendship to belong to. His days with Rembrandt had convinced him that friendship was the only means to make a man's stay on earth bearable. His new religion would allow friends to change their faces and their convictions as often as they wished as long as it was all in good faith. It would be the birthright of all to live as equals under the wide blue sky. The wealth of a man's parents would have no bearing on his own fortune. Likewise, the place of a man's birth would mean nothing. A man would not be expected to give an account of his private thoughts to his superiors because no one would be superior to another. A man's right to friendship on earth would be taken for granted by all the followers of this religion, and they would offer it to each other daily until the end of their lives.

The Polish Jews in the warehouse could care less about Samuel's ban from the Sephardic synagogue, or his lack of funds because he was an outcast. As far as they were concerned he was no different from the rest of them. So what if Samuel wasn't admitted into the Grand Synagogue? Neither were they. So what if Samuel was considered blasphemous? So were they, for being poor, unwashed, coarse, and uneducated. So what if Samuel had no money in his pockets? Neither did they. If Samuel risked expulsion from Amsterdam by the burgomasters, their situation was no different. Each of them risked expulsion from Amsterdam if he sold his wares outside the prescribed alleys or begged without a permit.

The Jews in the warehouse were also changing their perceptions of the world—although their reasons differed from

Samuel's. Samuel had opened his heart to the exigencies of his own soul through his friendship with Rembrandt. The indigent Jews in the warehouse had altogether another reason; they were convinced that their long-awaited Messiah had arrived. They were certain that he would deliver them from their misery and poverty and install them in their rightful homeland in the Holy Land.

Since the news of the Messiah's ascendance to his spiritual throne had been brought to Amsterdam, there was a swelling tide of hope and rejoicing. The warehouse hummed every night with talk and prayers. Where men used to gather around the pancake makers, now they gathered around the men who read from the new liturgy of hope. The zealous new converts fasted as often and as long as they could and flagellated themselves with branches or odd pieces of wood from the warehouse. A number of them formed a group to walk to the dunes on the outskirts of Amsterdam on Monday and Thursday evenings to bathe solemnly in the cold North Sea. They believed that these acts of self-purification would hasten the arrival of the time of miracles.

Amsterdam's burgomasters and Jewish notables had tried to suppress the news of the Messiah, but the Jewish traders and Dutch trade agents stationed in ports such as Smyrna and Constantinople in the Lands of the Turk had been supplying a steady stream of reports of this glorious saviour. A Dutch agent in Smyrna had unwittingly been one of the major sources of information for the Jews of Amsterdam. Feeling exceptionally lonely in Smyrna among the members of the French and English delegation who were given to much partying and drunkenness, this austere Calvinist had sought solace in writing detailed reports of his days in Smyrna to his family members in Amsterdam. His brother, a merchant dealing in spices and dried figs had been especially delighted to repeat the bizarre events his brother described in his letters. It so happened that this man had a Jewish business partner and several trusted Jewish workers with whom he spent much time in conversation. From mouth to mouth the wondrous news travelled, and however much they were exaggerated, all who relayed them knew that the stories about the Messiah could never approximate the deeds of the Messiah.

He had circled Jerusalem on a white horse seven times like a king, before entering it for the first time. It was said that the Christians and Muslims as well as the Jews of the Holy City had greeted him with joy. He was so full of ecstasy when he prayed that he often levitated and hovered above the congregation. His closest friends and followers were also blessed with such weightlessness. Some had been sent on clouds to faraway lands as messengers, across the river Sambatyon, to herald the arrival of the Messiah to the lost tribes. Sabbatai Sevi was his name, and he was already called "Querido," "Beloved," for he was loved with a love that surpassed a mother's love for her child, a man's love for his wife, a child's love for his father. He had been entrusted with the keys to the souls of everyone, whether beggar, wealthy merchant, or simple journeyman.

Jews from places as far away as Brazil and India wrote to him, pleading with him to reveal the roots of their souls, for he was able to do so by merely repeating aloud the name of the petitioner. He cured infertility, reversed the course of fatal illnesses, restored sight to the blind, hearing to the deaf, helped return lost objects to their rightful owners, joined lovers parted by misunderstandings, took away the stubborn pains of grief from hearts and replaced them with the warmth of hope.

When the astounding news reached Amsterdam that, during one of his exalted states, the Messiah had walked in the streets of Smyrna, his native city, while holding a large dead fish swaddled in white linen as if it were a baby, many of his followers in Amsterdam did the same. As herring was abundant and cheap in

Amsterdam, affordable even to the residents of the warehouse, many zealous believers slept with fish swaddled in linens beside their heads to be close to their Messiah even during their sleep. The Messiah had carried the fish in his arms because the sign of Pisces was now under the influence of Saturn, and it was now, as predicted in the secret scriptures, that a Messiah would overcome the rule of the skeptics who dominated the synagogues. The Messiah had been exiled from his native city for announcing the time of miracles, as was also prophesied, and had begun his travels as a fish will travel the seas of the world, never resting, never predictable.

His followers, however poor, gave alms because they believed that alms cast into the world would assist the Messiah during his travels. As bread crumbs cast into the sea will feed anonymous fish, alms given freely would sustain the helpers of the Messiah; for who can tell from the start who has been assigned to be a helper? By keeping open the channels of giving and taking through which beggars and visionaries survive in the world, the alms givers believed that the Messiah would encounter more people along the way who would open their hearts to him.

On the evening of the day the pilgrims departed from the warehouse on a journey to Jerusalem the angel Sealiah appeared to Samuel again. Despite Samuel's warnings that this journey could not be completed so easily on foot, considering that there were many wars and bandits and hostile governments along the way; not to mention difficult mountain passes, snowstorms, wild animals, peasants who spoke ferocious foreign tongues that contained no words common to French, German, English, Polish, Dutch, or Spanish, the converts had insisted that they would be helped by those who had heard the message of the Messiah, for he speaks to hearts without the aid of languages. After they left the remaining residents of the warehouse prayed together in the weak green light of their lanterns and asked for the manifestation of miracles that were their due. A sense of peace pervaded the place, more so than usual.

Samuel was almost asleep, enjoying the first precious moments of silence after the humming of prayers had subsided, and after the beggars had finished sharing out their daily earnings to please the spirit of the Messiah. Although the wind gusted through the gaps in the walls inadequately blocked by haphazardly placed planks, the warehouse still stank of rotting fish and old rags. It was surprising then to smell something as fresh as the woods on a spring day: a whiff of pine resin and wild mint with a hint of anise. Samuel sniffed the fresh scent and breathed deeply before opening his eyes. Shrouded in green light, a tall figure stood over him. Samuel smiled.

"Sealiah?"

"Yes, my son. You called me today."

Sealiah spoke with a voice that resembled a sudden blast of wind, as if a long closed door had been opened in Samuel's ears.

"I did?"

"When you sent the pilgrims off today, you did."

"I don't recall thinking of you, but if you say I did, I must have."

"It's time for you to leave as well."

"To Jerusalem?"

Sealiah was quiet.

"Where then?"

"You'll find out soon, in due time. But first you must complete a task you have been neglecting."

"What is it?"

"You still have that paper in your pocket."

Samuel reached into the breast pocket of his jacket. In the recesses of his pocket, softened by time and the dampness of his body, it lay there, the tulip stock. He had forgotten about it.

"You think I'll get something for it?"

Sealiah nodded. "It's time to ask for expert help."

"Then I will."

Samuel saw Sealiah smile as the green light surrounding him became warmer.

"Don't go yet, please. Who are you, exactly?"

Samuel heard the floorboards creak.

"I am an angel."

"Why are you here, then? I am not a vegetable."

"Your fate is tied to vegetables."

"Are tulips vegetables?"

"To me, they are. I will help you with the tulips."

"Tell me something."

"Yes?"

"Do you rule over onions as well, then?"

"And etrogs. I'm done, now."

"Will you come back?"

"I am always with you, son." With that the green light diminished in size and, when it was almost imperceptible, it lingered a good while over Samuel's heart before disappearing completely.

As Samuel fell into a deep sleep, he wondered why an angel had chosen to help him. It was a mystery, but he felt properly guided by this angel of vegetables.

Captain One-Leg promised to bring in a profit for Samuel, as well as a nice a cut for himself, if Samuel dared to trust him with his tulip stock. Not that Captain One-Leg was completely trust-worthy, but he was a frequent visitor to the warehouse, and he wasn't going to swindle a friend of his cronies. Samuel was sure of this. A man needs a friend whatever his station in life.

In addition, Captain One-Leg was easily identifiable. He had a unique face with a distinctive scar running lengthwise across his right cheek. He was proud of that gash and often showed off the knife that had caused it, a vicious looking blade with a whalebone handle which had several notches on its side. The small notch was for his own face, he said. "That's when the knife became mine. The owner of the knife, last I saw him, he was lying in front of a tavern somewhere in the West Indies." His swaggering gait, all the more exaggerated because of his wooden leg, added to his reputation for mischief which preceded him in every quarter of Amsterdam, long before the somber beat of his stump resounded on the cobblestones.

Captain One-Leg claimed inside knowledge of the stock exchange through his friends at the coffee houses on Kalverstraat, whose business was to spy on merchants and traders who patronized those places. Merchants were the best source to predict the future of stocks. They were always discussing among themselves which commodities were in great supply and therefore bound to become cheaper, which were more in demand, but scarcely stocked, and which were not yet fashionable but on their way to becoming highly desirable, and therefore valuable.

"Now tulip stocks are tulip stocks and everyone knows what tulips are, there is no mystery to this commodity, but the timing is important. When to sell and who to sell to. That, my friend, is the trick," said Captain One leg, as he grabbed the musty piece of paper bearing Senor DaCosta's spidery handwriting and several oversized numerals.

Spring brought more sunshine and people ventured outdoors more. The wider streets bustled with vendors and strollers, and in the narrower alleys children chased hoops and struck balls with kolf sticks. Shopkeepers stepped outside to smoke their pipes in the slow hours of the afternoon when business was lax. Older men with nothing to do set up makeshift tables on the sunny side of streets by doorways away from the traffic and played cards. Young women gathered in threes and fours to gossip and catch the attention of potential suitors passing by on barges in the canals.

Samuel wandered the city, wearing the same old clothes, but with a simple Dutchman's white cap instead of the old cap the fishmonger had given him the day he left the DaCosta residence. His appearance was now indistinguishable from the scores of indigent men who walked in the city, at times looking for odd jobs, at times begging or vending a sack of rags, a bunch of turnips, or a stack of salted herring. Although he no longer looked like a foreigner in Amsterdam, he more than ever felt like one.

Samuel continued to visit Rembrandt, but more to chat at the end of the day when natural light had waned and prevented an artist from sketching and engraving. Rembrandt was no longer interested in having Samuel model for him. He assured Samuel that he had sketched enough and was now preparing a number of engraving plates from the numerous sketches he had made. Through the months Samuel had become accustomed to the artist's secretive behaviour and did not press him with questions about his current project. He was certain that he figured in whatever it was, for he had modeled in almost all of Rembrandt's sketches during the last eight months.

One evening in late May, when Samuel had gone to visit Rembrandt, he encountered a loutish bunch of men in Rembrandt's backyard, drinking foreign ale from a cask that looked a century old. As he stepped into the backyard, Samuel saw to his horror that one of the men was in the process of urinating into the canal. Rembrandt, himself quite drunk, did not seem to find this objectionable.

"Come and meet some of your own people," shouted Rembrandt, with uncharacteristic expansiveness.

Samuel was taken aback. What did Rembrandt believe he had in common with these loud boors?

"These are the etrog agents I was telling you about."

Samuel nodded formally to acknowledge them. The fellow who was urinating had returned with his fly half unbuttoned. He wiped his hand on his pants and offered it to Samuel. Samuel declined the greeting. An uncomfortable silence fell over the group, which was promptly broken by the eldest of the three visitors.

"Come sit down, brother," he said, patting the seat of the empty chair next to him.

Samuel strode over to the chair and settled down, feeling trapped. The old man offered him a pewter mug filled to the brim with the foreign brew.

"Have a sip, brother, it will take the chill off your bones."

The two others smiled smugly.

Defiantly, Samuel emptied half of the mug in one gulp and set it down for all to acknowledge his feat. As the men gasped in disbelief, Samuel could barely contain himself in his seat, so strong was his urge to throw himself into the canal to cool the flames that were rising from his gut.

"Lion's milk, that is what you had, brother. You've proven to us once again that lions are quiet creatures."

Samuel could barely move his lips to grimace.

"Say, doesn't he remind you of our friend Ali?" remarked the fellow whose hand Samuel had declined to shake.

"Sure does. The same expression on his long face, all right. Could be brothers," concurred the third man.

"Did you go to the same school where they teach you how to be dignified even when you are drunk?" asked the other.

"Leave the poor fellow alone, till he comes out of the lion's den," said the oldest one.

Soon, Samuel could inhale. He took a deep breath to quell the flames. A warm buzzing enveloped his head. He didn't mind it at all. He found it pleasant. He had never felt this warm since his arrival in Amsterdam.

The five men continued to drink in the backyard that was transformed into a Mediterranean garden by the ale they all shared. Samuel reconsidered his initial judgement of these people and decided they were not objectionable. In fact, they were quite amicable.

All three men were Jews from the same village on the eastern coast of the Adriatic sea. They traveled back and forth between the ports of the Ottoman Empire and the ports of Western Europe, selling and buying, trading in both exotic and staple goods. They were proud to hold all of the Western European etrog trade in their hands. They attributed their success in trade to their unfailing method. First, they confirmed the quantity of etrog demanded by the wholesalers in ports such as Hamburg and Amsterdam, then they traveled back to the island of Corfu where the etrogs were cultivated by the Corfiote Jews there. After registering their cargo with the Venetian agents on the island of Corfu, they sailed to Constantinople to pick up other goods sold by the Levantine merchants of the Ottoman Empire. There, they also informed the Venetian and Ottoman agents of the exact list of their cargo and the quantities they were committed to carrying on their voyage west and what and how much they expected to bring back on their return voyage.

What they also did, and perhaps this was the most important ingredient of their success, was that they worked out the precise route they intended to navigate and left the particulars with the various customs brokers and agents in Constantinople to insure themselves against any mishaps due to military skirmishes in the Mediterranean, or worse, to pirates working for their own gain. These men had friends all over the Mediterranean and the Ottoman Empire. Among them, they spoke a total of twelve languages and their dialects, including Turkish and Albanian, as well as Spanish, Portuguese, French, German, and Dutch.

They were surprised to learn that Samuel had traveled as much as he had, and that he was friends with Rembrandt when he could have chosen to remain in the upper class Sephardic Jewish circle of Amsterdam. They laughed aloud when they found out Samuel had been educated by the Jesuits. It was already past midnight and a deep chill had descended on the backyard along with an ink-black darkness, when they discovered that their friend Ali and Samuel had attended the same seminary.

Samuel sat up in his chair, as alert as he could be under the influence of "lion's milk", and asked them if they knew what their friend Ali was called when he was at Alcala.

"Why, Alonzo, of course," responded the eldest.

The other two laughed for what seemed an interminably long time, until they could answer Samuel, who kept asking, "How old is this Alonzo?"

"About your age, but who can tell, he speaks like a very wise man, but he has a young wife, not even twenty, and two little babies."

"Alonzo has children?"

The men laughed again. "Good looking ones, too," said the youngest of them.

"No surprise," said the other, "you've seen the beauty he married. How he managed that, I don't know."

"Her uncle offered her to Ali, because they didn't want him to leave."

"The old man at the customs office that Ali works with is her uncle?"

Samuel was now wide awake. "Do you know what his family name was when he was in Alcala?"

"Ali? We only know him as Ali Captain, or Ali Effendi, like every honorable Turk is called," answered the eldest one.

The men started laughing again. "A good Turk, he is, for sure, ha ha, ha ha."

"Didn't Ali mention he was once called Melami?" asked the one who had pissed into the canal.

"Melami?" Samuel cried hoarsely. "My best friend!"

"You know him?" asked the third one. The others, too, seemed shaken. "You know our friend Ali? Now look at fate; this is nothing but the hand of fate. From where to where, boys."

"Ali won't believe we met his friend in Amsterdam," said the eldest. "Thanks to Ali, we now have another friend in Amsterdam."

"Will you tell him, I miss him greatly?" asked Samuel. "Better yet, will you take a letter to him?"

"As long as it is not sealed, we'll take it to him. We can't risk carrying anything that might be considered seditious."

"That's fine, that's perfectly fine with me. I wasn't intending to seal anything. I don't even have a seal. Do I look like a man who owns a seal?" Samuel was gibbering now.

"That's fine with us, but you have to give us the letter now, because we intend to leave Amsterdam good and early tomorrow, don't we, boys?"

"That's fine with me, too," said Samuel. "Why don't we all

move inside, and I'll compose a letter while you catch a bit of sleep. But first, let's put our host to bed."

They had all forgotten about Rembrandt who was dozing in his chair with a half-empty mug on the floor beside him. Together, they heaved Rembrandt from his chair and lay him in his bed. The men each found themselves a corner and settled immediately into sleep, betraying years of practice in such arrangements. As for Samuel, he rummaged through Rembrandt's stack of sketching papers and found a thin sheet with a smooth surface. As the three traders snored, Samuel sat down at the large table in the kitchen by the sputtering flame of the oil lamp. He wrote a short, but loving letter to his friend Alonzo with Rembrandt's scratchy reed pen.

Early in June Captain One-Leg sold Samuel's tulip stock at the most profitable price, just as he had promised. He had waited for the stock prices to rise, following the rumors of a shortage in healthy bulbs in quality varieties. He had made good use of his spies in the coffeehouses of Kalverstraat, where these false rumors were created and circulated by shrewd traders who speculated in bulb futures. The rumour was highly plausible to anyone who did not have inside knowledge of the market. A number of skirmishes had taken place that spring and summer between the Barbary and Christian pirates sailing the Mediterranean. Since both parties raided merchant ships regardless of the banners they traveled under, a general state of anxiety had pervaded the stock market of Amsterdam. Traders were inclined to be much more conservative in their dealings with international deals and more susceptible to rumors of expected shortages of domestic crops.

On just such a day of mercantile anxiety exaggerated by the overcast sky, which sagged with heavy grey clouds that grazed the pointed hats of the traders at the bourse without delivering any relief in rain, Captain One-Leg scored a miracle with Samuel's stock, selling it for 30 guilders, about fifteen minutes before the bourse closed promptly at two o'clock. He kept five guilders for himself, a handsome margin of profit, no doubt, but all would agree that it was well deserved, considering his adroit handling of the sale.

The money brought immense relief to Samuel, who could now conceive of altering his life circumstances considerably. When Captain One-Leg handed him his earnings across from the warehouse out of earshot of its residents, Samuel could hardly believe his eyes that counted the notes before his fingers touched them. He carefully folded the one five guilder and two ten guilder notes into a small square and pinned the packet to the fabric deep inside the breast pocket of his jacket where the tulip stock had once lain crumpled and forgotten.

Before they parted Captain One-Leg advised Samuel to keep quiet about the money. "Why tempt the devil," he said, "for his eminence resides in all of us." He winked and tapped Samuel on the foot with his crutch before hobbling down the street. Halfway down the block he turned and put his palm up in the air as a farewell and a greeting, but most certainly as a reminder for silence; for once business is successfully completed it is best not mentioned.

Although Samuel remained tight-lipped about the money with his friends at the warehouse, he confided in Rembrandt about his good fortune and spoke about the new decisions that now confronted him.

Rembrandt urged him to wait until the etrog traders returned. "Perhaps they will bring you news of your friend," he said. "You might consider visiting your friend, or seeking employment with the agents, for example. They are men of your own kind, Samuel; men who can travel in both Jewish and Christian lands while keeping a home and hearth in the land of the Turk."

"That's where they differ," countered Samuel.

Rembrandt responded wisely that the land of the Turk might be an alternative for him as well. "You could at least visit your friend Alonzo and see for yourself. You probably wouldn't have to spend any money to get there, either."

"How?" asked Samuel, puzzled. When he was a Jesuit the church had paid for him; and when he was a Jew the synagogue had borne the cost of his living; but as a free man, devoid of links to the church, the synagogue, or the state, why would anyone pay for his travel expenses to visit the land of the Turk?

"Offer your services as a scribe to the captain of the ship that the etrog traders travel on," suggested Rembrandt. "Offer to help with the ship logs and whatever else may be needed for the return journey to Constantinople. They will feed you and show you a corner to lie down at night. They might even give you a bunk of your own in a cabin so that you don't have to sleep exposed to the elements on the deck. Those ships are always in need of a good scribe, but few learned men apply for work on them. It's certain you'll get a job with them if you ask."

The idea was a good one, and like all good ideas that are meant to become realities, it stayed with Samuel comfortably and gave him peace of mind and the certainty that this was how his life would unfold. He no longer thought of the letter from Alonzo in terms of "if" it might arrive, but "when" it would arrive. The letter would certainly bear an invitation from his dear friend Alonzo, now called Ali, to visit him in Constantinople, the birthplace of the tulip which had made this dream possible in the first place.

In late June, after a day spent wandering in the countryside along the dikes on the outskirts of Amsterdam, Samuel came back to the warehouse for an afternoon nap. The weather was warm so few people stayed indoors at the warehouse, and a late afternoon nap could be enjoyed without an interruption. Samuel curled up in his corner, now distinctly and comfortably his own after months of inhabitation. The tightly packed hay which formed his pallet smelled of his own body, and his wool hat and large green overcoat, which he had no use for during the summer months, lay in a soft musty heap next to the small tin bowl and wooden spoon with which he sometimes drank soup at night from the common pot.

He stretched lazily on his pallet, indulging in the warmth still in his muscles from the leisurely walk in the countryside, throughout which the sun had shined graciously. He yawned and waited for the cozy weariness to take over and deliver him into a restful nap. His thoughts wandered to his friend Alonzo, as they often did since his encounter with the etrog salesmen. Because he was so relaxed a question he had not previously allowed himself to entertain popped into his mind. He wondered whether Alonzo had remained a Jesuit in Constantinople. If Alonzo was married with children, he could no longer be a practicing Jesuit.

Samuel was distressed by the possibility that his friend had also converted, perhaps to Islam. Why had he not thought of this before? If he had converted so readily to Judaism in Amsterdam, what stopped Alonzo from becoming a Mohammedan in the land of the Turk? Or what if Alonzo had been won over by Sabbatai Sevi? Now that was even more difficult to swallow. Could Alonzo be among the frenzied disciples of the self-declared messiah? Samuel admitted that he had grown up with Alonzo and studied with him, but he had no means of predicting what Alonzo might do as a mature man in a foreign land whose customs were so different from the European countries they had lived in together. He regretted not having asked the etrog salesmen about Alonzo's current beliefs.

How hard would it be for Alonzo to drop that armour of belief which they had once been assured was strong enough to deflect the contradictory and puzzling questions that the common men would hurl at them like spears? What had happened to Alonzo; what were the circumstances that had changed him? Was it riches, was it the beauty of an Oriental woman that had melted his heart? During their years at the seminary, they had been assiduously prepared against precisely these temptations.

As he was contemplating these questions Samuel felt so warm that he believed somehow this was the reason for Alonzo's change of heart. It must have been the warmth of the Middle East that made Alonzo's old beliefs irrelevant. Samuel imagined the warmth of the sun in Constantinople, how he would sit on a sun-warmed boulder by the sea, next to Alonzo, just as if they were boys again, with the minarets of mosques piercing the sky in the horizon. The church bells were ringing, because there were also many churches in Constantinople, when he heard his voice called.

"Samuel!"

Thinking it was Alonzo calling his name, he turned toward the door of the warehouse.

It was Sealiah.

"You're back."

"Yes," said, Sealiah, "but not for long. I will travel with you some more, but soon, you'll be going to a place where you won't need me as much."

That did not sound propitious to Samuel. "You said you'd always be with me," he responded dejectedly. He felt like a child about to be abandoned by his father.

"I admit I gave you my word. And I will be with you, always, but soon you'll change lands and live where other angels reign. I have already informed them about you. They will be closer to you there and come to your aid faster than I can."

"So, you're staying here?" asked Samuel.

"And you're leaving."

"You're sure?"

"You need a new name for your journey," continued Sealiah, ignoring Samuel's question. "I'll give you mine."

"Your name? I'm a mortal, not an angel," answered Samuel rationally.

"You'll have a man's name, to suit your new life. You'll be called Salih."

"Salih?"

"Serviceable, good, pious. That's you, your new name."

"Salih?"

"Salih Effendi." Sealiah laughed audibly. "An effendi, like a good Turk."

"Salih," repeated Samuel compulsively.

"Not bad is it? Suits you, son; it suits you well. It will bring you peace. Salih Effendi?"

Samuel was surprised to see himself respond to that name. "Yes?"

"The name will help you exercise your tongue."

"It's not a difficult name."

Sealiah smiled. "It's not the name that will improve your tongue, but the new man with that name. It is time for you to take your tongue out of its sheath. But use it well, use it for prayer, as a ladder to ascend to your true self. For when badly used, the tongue is a knife that cuts the rungs of that ladder. Are you listening, Salih Effendi?"

Samuel blinked. When he opened his eyes, he saw Sealiah hopping up a ladder that rose past the roof of the warehouse. The lower rungs disappeared in quick succession as Sealiah left them behind.

Sealiah? For the first time, Samuel noticed the "aliah," the Hebrew word for "ascension" that was embedded in Sealiah's name. Yes, his tongue was moving differently already, tasting the hidden meanings of words behind the obvious ones. Samuel was ready to become Salih Effendi.

In the first week of August, far in advance of the Feast of Tabernacles, the etrog salesmen returned to Amsterdam bearing a letter from Ali Effendi. They dropped it off at Rembrandt's house before continuing on their itinerary to deliver etrogs to all the synagogues and wealthy families in the Jewish communities of western Europe. The traders were in ebullient spirits. The crop in Corfu had been plentiful that year, yielding larger than usual fruit which were also less sour than in previous years. The agents were thus assured of high profits, which they were anxious to increase by scheduling one more business trip between the east and the west before the winter arrived.

Hearing this, Rembrandt suggested that they take Samuel along on their return trip to Constantinople and employ him as their accountant and scribe. The oldest agent responded favorably to the suggestion. "We'll take him, all right, but he has to wash himself thoroughly and step into a change of clothes before I let him touch my ledgers."

Imagining Samuel clean and transformed into the scholar he had once been, but this time on board a ship nervously pacing the length of a narrow deck, struck them all as hilarious. They laughed heartily when the youngest trader imitated a nervous Samuel searching for a place to hide away from the world, burrowing his head under a mound of spare sails.

"He'll do well," said the oldest one. "The poor man needs to be given a chance to earn his living among ordinary folk, that's all."

"As ordinary as you all," responded Rembrandt.

"As ordinary as our etrogs." They howled with laughter again.

When Samuel saw his full name, Samuel Salvador, carefully written in precisely formed letters on the large envelope, he was convinced that Alonzo had remained the same although he was now a married man working as a customs broker in Constantinople. When he turned the envelope to open it, however, he wondered whether he had been too hasty in his judgement. The royal blue wax seal at the back of the envelope was the kind usually preferred by unschooled merchants with lofty social aspirations. Had Alonzo changed this much? The Alonzo that Samuel knew as a young man was someone who would value reserve over ostentation. Perhaps this was the only sealing wax available in Constantinople.

But what was Samuel to make of the seal? A large "A", shaped more like a grotesque horseshoe than a proper letter was deeply impressed upon the blue wax. Over the burrow of the right stem of the letter which ended in a sweeping curly flourish, the wax had been stretched and splattered, creating a distasteful mess resembling a bird dropping. How had the same Alonzo whose neatness and meticulousness once irritated even their most compulsive teachers at the seminary, allowed himself to send an envelope in this condition?

When he opened the envelope Samuel was reassured. His friend had not changed beyond recognition. Mercifully, his handwriting had remained more or less the same, although it was noticeably sloppier. All his words leaned to the left for a few lines, then they sloped to the right, and back again to the left, as though Alonzo had changed his mind frequently while he wrote, or worse, didn't care. At the seminary Alonzo had been the only student in Samuel's class who could take down a whole lecture verbatim and still receive praises on his calligraphy. His letters were spidery now. Samuel surmised that it was not because the nib of his pen was thinner, or his ink more diluted.

Although Alonzo was now Ali Effendi, he had chosen to write his letter in Spanish, the language of their youth at the seminary. After a few quick formal salutations at the beginning, Alonzo had dispensed with all the customary rules for epistolary form and plunged into a passionate invitation to Samuel.

"Come and experience true brotherhood and sharing," he wrote.

> Here, you'll never feel the pangs of solitude. Constantinople is a jewel among cities. It is the gathering place of free thinkers, rebels, inventors. Come here. You'll find employment, plenty of companionship. The air is a lot easier to breathe, and life, overall, is more pleasant. There are lush gardens to wander in and sonorous fountains to rest by. You will be able to study as you please and accumulate material wealth as well as knowledge. You will converse with the best minds of our century. Gentle and fair women will gladly serve you.
>
> The customs of the Turks are different, but they are moral people, concerned with justice in everyday life. They believe in fate, but not in original sin. They consider Jesus and Moses equally holy and will appeal to them for miracles in addition to Mohammed. Virgin Mary is known as Mother Miriam here and the Turks and Christians alike honour her with equal reverence.
>
> The land of the Turks is like Spain. The heartland in Anatolia is as big as Spain and has the same number of people. It too guards one side of the Mediterranean. Even the climate is the same as Spain. The country is rich in

minerals and foodstuffs. The Muslims are as tolerant toward people of different creeds as once they were in Spain. The Turks are in need of able traders, scribes, and accountants. You may safely prosper here. You will eat the same fruits you savored as a child; only here, they are bigger and tastier.

As you read this letter, I can imagine you doubting me. But let me tell you what I have learned: it is fear that blocks the hearts of men, my brother. It is the ignorance of the divine light that shines into all our hearts. Come free your heart from its weights, come to the land of light. For a man must travel through all the religions of the world to understand the common destiny of man. The light of redemption has to be filtered through all the possible prisms that the human soul can provide. Come hasten the arrival of the messiah that will be a messiah to us all, by learning once more, another way to be a believer.

After reiterating his invitation to Samuel to join him in Constantinople, Alonzo had signed his new name with a confident signature. Samuel noted that over the "A" of Ali, Alonzo had added an accent as if it were an extra roof, an added shelter, or a turban that increased the eminence of an already high forehead.

Samuel was now convinced that it was time to leave the city of water to travel to the city of light. In Portugal and Spain he had lived in cities of earth. He had left them for Amsterdam, the city of water, and now it was time to try inhabiting another element. If Alonzo claimed Constantinople was the city of light then it was also a city of air and fire, for what else is light composed of? If he went to Constantinople, he would indeed complete the alchemical requisites for the total transformation of his soul.

Light he needed, for at the beginning there was light, and with light, there would be words and conversation. With conversation, there may be conversion, but Ali would guide him through the process.

Samuel did not have much to do to prepare himself for his journey. With his earnings from the sale of the tulip stock, he purchased a new set of clothes, a spare linen shirt and a change of breeches. He left these at Rembrandt's house for safekeeping in his new travelling satchel. In the satchel he placed the three books he had kept throughout his various journeys and jobs: the Old and the New Testaments, and a tattered copy of Aesop's fables in Latin. He soon added a fourth book. As a parting present, Rembrandt gave him a copy of Menasseh ben Israel's *Piedra Gloriosa O, de la Estatua de Nebuchadnesar*, which contained four of his etchings. Despite Rembrandt's insistence that he take it for free, Samuel also purchased a print of the engraving Rembrandt had made of his back in front of the synagogue. Rembrandt asked him why he wanted that particular work of all the sketches he had modeled for him.

"That is the only completed engraving I have of you; true, but it is also the only one that doesn't show your face. Wouldn't you rather have a sketch of your face, or any sketch where your profile is discernible? Don't you want to take along a souvenir of your time in Amsterdam?"

"In Europe I have been faceless," replied Samuel gravely. "I will carry this picture to remind myself of that."

"You think the land of the Turk will give you a face?"

"Perhaps it will offer me a few of them," responded Samuel.

"I gave you a few faces, myself," said Rembrandt, assertively.

"No," said Samuel, "you repeated the same face on different

bodies."

"How so?" asked Rembrandt, appalled.

"Because you never varied my stare," Samuel responded. "In all your pictures of me, I always appear humbly uncertain of my purpose, whether I am gazing at the sky, at another face, or at an imaginary viewer who is staring at me. I am never determined in your pictures. I always appear puzzled; as if I have just realized that my human limitations are insurmountable."

Rembrandt was speechless. Could his model be the first man to understand what he had been trying to do with his art all his life? But Samuel was fighting for himself, not for Rembrandt. Hadn't he encouraged Samuel to do just that? He had told Samuel what it takes to survive as an artist, and now Samuel was putting his teachings to a different use.

It was obvious that Samuel wanted a place where he could express the contradictions of his nature openly. And according to Samuel the place which could accommodate so much contradiction was not art, but another land. This wasn't quite what Rembrandt had envisioned as Samuel's salvation. He had merely thought that a change of air in the land of the Turk would do Samuel good, that a restful sojourn to visit an old friend would cure him of his melancholy state and bring out his true nature. Samuel, on the other hand, was ready to subvert the principles that made a European man live, produce, and reproduce within reason.

"I don't want to be inhuman," said Samuel, gently, backtracking.

"Superhuman perhaps?"

"No, on the contrary, I want to be thoroughly human. To be human is to passionately desire irreconcilable things in irreconcilable ways. I want to go someplace where I can desire without shame and where I can believe that what I desire at that moment is to last forever."

"Although you might change your mind?" said Rembrandt.

"Although I might change my mind only to desire once again, just as passionately as before."

Samuel carefully inserted the print depicting his back in front of the synagogue into the book Rembrandt had given him. The loose print nestled comfortably among the other Rembrandt prints bound into the book: The vision of Ezechiel, the Statue of Nebuchadnezzar, David and Goliath, and Jacob's Ladder.

On his last night in Amsterdam Samuel was given a musical sendoff by his friends at the warehouse. The warehouse was now exclusively inhabited by the disciples of Sabbatai Sevi. Although Samuel had never openly declared his allegiance to the messiah, the fact that he was leaving for Constantinople, where the messiah was now imprisoned for challenging the throne of the Turkish Sultan, was interpreted as a mystery whose true intent would be revealed in due time. Samuel neither accepted nor rejected their interpretation of his journey. He did not wish to alienate the people who had shared the same roof with him for a year.

His friends gathered at the centre of the warehouse where they habitually read from the messianic scriptures. After distributing a bowl of soup to each of the residents, as was their new custom as followers of Sabbatai Sevi, they started singing. They chanted songs of love and joy, of suffering and redemption, of the birth pangs of light in the womb of darkness, and of the mystery of the light that is dispersed into myriad shards in the souls of men. "How to gather this diffused light, and make it whole, sweet Lord, teach us," they wailed and sobbed openly, like children.

Because they loved Samuel, and because Samuel was going to the city where the source of their light was now imprisoned, they sang the song that Sabbatai Sevi liked best. The old Castilian love song, Meliselda, was reputed to be the messiah's favorite song. He had sung it often in synagogue services, reading many mysteries into it. The heresy of this act and the beauty of the song had been reported in many letters written from the Levant. Eventually the song itself had made its way to the west, where it had originated. It was reborn in the west after being smuggled across borders in the memories of believers and on rolls of music sheets sewn into the hems of jackets. In the warehouse, Meliselda sounded doubly mysterious in the mouths of the Eastern European Jews who did not speak Spanish. With a refrain of Meliselda still on their lips, the singers embraced each other.

When Samuel went to his pallet at the warehouse for the last time he felt that his departure wasn't a loss to the warehouse residents. But then, neither was it a gain. He planned to rise early the next morning, walk over to Rembrandt's house, wash himself, change into his new set of clothes, and leave Amsterdam with the etrog merchants who would come to meet him there. He stretched on his pallet and clasped his hands under his head, resting his neck comfortably in the centre of his intertwined fingers.

In his dream Senhor Torcato caught up with him in the long corridor linking the orphanage refectory to the chapel. He smiled cynically, pouting his carmine lips. "The dean has just informed me that we will be dispatching you to Alcala in the summer," he declared. Samuel wished he could have kept the news of his departure a secret until the last day. But he had no control over the dissemination of personal information at the orphanage. None of the boys did. His life was everyone's business, especially Senhor Torcato's. Nothing could escape his prying ears tuned to hear the faintest of whispers.

Senhor Torcato craned his head and hissed into Samuel's neck. "You can't run away from your troubles, my boy. You will always take them with you."

Samuel knew Senhor Torcato was telling the truth. Although it was an honour to be chosen to study at the seminary at Alcala, it also meant a continuation of the routines that suffocated him in Portugal. Going away would not change much. He would probably meet others like Senhor Torcato, perhaps worse.

"Even if you change your tongue, speak another language, you will repeat the same things," hissed Senhor Torcato.

It was true that a man's destiny cannot be changed by speaking another tongue. Samuel felt thoroughly deflated. But there was also a note of envy concealed in his teacher's remarks. Samuel quickly reassessed Senhor Torcato's warning. He was much younger than Senhor Torcato, and Senhor Torcato envied him for it. Above all, he envied Samuel's belief that he could make a fresh start by going away.

Emboldened, Samuel shot back: "Perhaps I have things to say that can only be spoken in particular parts of the world in unique languages. Perhaps, I will observe and collect things that are not to be translated, but savored as they are, within the one language they belong."

Hearing this, Senhor Torcato's lips dropped. But he had to get the last word in, as always. Gathering his composure, he replied caustically, "The tongue has no bones, but the earth has ears, my son." His fat lips stretched in a vindictive grin.

Samuel closed his eyes. He refused to stare at Senhor Torcato's face. He had had enough of such bitterness. When Senhor Torcato turned to walk away from Samuel, his robe swished around his legs. Samuel continued to stand in the marble corridor with his eyes shut tight. When Senhor Torcato's footsteps died away, and Samuel could no longer hear echoes of his teacher's angry gait beyond the chapel door which had closed behind him, a sudden gust of wind unlatched the casement of the window beside Samuel. Fresh air and sunshine poured into the corridor.

❖

Samuel stood on the deck of a galleon on a bright sunny day, entering the harbour of Constantinople. Despite the noon heat, a fresh northern breeze blowing down the strait of Bosphorus refreshed him. The large white sails of the galleon billowed and fluttered above him against the wide-open blue sky. Several large sea gulls were keeping pace with the steady advance of the ship, circling just ahead of its prow. They flapped their wings to adjust themselves to the forward moving air current so that they seemed to glide toward the harbour to announce the approach of the city of light that Samuel had chosen to come to.

Samuel saw the silhouette of thin minarets in the direction the birds pointed with their beaks. When they flapped their wings again, the horizon shifted, and rolling emerald hills claimed Samuel's vision so that he knew that in this city the sky was free of buildings in parts. The sea gulls shrieked again, and Samuel saw red tiled roofs lining the sinuous bend of paths down the hills, and streets by the edge of the water shaded by wide oak trees flushed with leaves.

The sea gulls descended, and Samuel saw that the water was busy with small boats, people coming and going in the boats, greeting and arguing, buying and selling. Young muscular men with shaved heads and long pointed moustaches were swimming in the water like carefree dolphins, racing with each other, climbing on and diving down from boats, and waving at the galleon from the water. More serious folk had gathered by the bridge at the mouth of the Golden Horn. Resting their elbows on the rails they quietly watched the new arrivals approach their city.

Among the turbaned men, could it be, could it be that Samuel saw his friend Alonzo Melami? "Alonzo, Alonzo, Ali, my friend, Ali Melami." Ali's head seemed to have grown longer, his forehead more exalted than the last time Samuel had seen him. Samuel thought that ironically, the shorter name and the strange headgear made Ali look taller and more dignified.

With the thick band of white muslin wrapped around its felt centre, Ali Melami's hat looked like a huge tulip in bloom. Samuel noted that as far as he could see on the bridge and on the streets along the shore, the whole city was populated by dignified men who carried large tulips on their heads. So, this was the land promised by Sealiah, the angel of flowers and vegetables!

A pack of dogs howled in the distant hills. A short sharp gust of wind lifted Samuel's white cap off his head and tumbled it into the water where Samuel watched it slowly sink by the side of the galleon. "Gone now, gone now, the old head," Samuel thought the sea gulls said, as they swirled by.

It was then Ali Melami saw Samuel on the deck of the ship and waved his arms in a wide languid sweep. Samuel saw him smile, and he knew his friend was happy, and rested, and content, and slower all around. He was happy for the happiness that belonged to his friend and the happiness that would belong to him in this city.

A call to prayer emanated from the minarets. Samuel saw a man standing on a tiny balcony at the side of one of the spires, praying aloud toward the wide open sky through his hands cupped around his mouth. The man sent the prayer to the heavens with the full vigour of his lungs. Some people heeded him and walked toward the mosque and some kept on doing what they were doing before—talking, arguing, swimming, laughing, or waving at a friend.

"You're here, you're here, you're here," the sea gulls seemed to be saying as they flapped their wings.

FIVE

The Messiah

THE PHONE is ringing again. It must be David's mother. I won't answer it.

Dear Ali,

It's been nearly four years since we last saw each other. I didn't write for a long time because I got caught up with my work, my new relationship, and a new city. Every day there is always something new to discover in the city, some extra paperwork because I'm a foreign student, and then, of course, all the books to read, articles to photocopy, papers to write.

In the last few months I've started thinking about who I was before I became an anthropology student and started living at Terrasse St. Denis. I'm not sure if I'm doing the right thing by living in Montreal, or by studying anthropology. It all seems like time off from the real life I should be leading, but I'm not sure exactly what that real life is supposed to be.

I know I felt very good, truly myself, when I was travelling, and I also know that I felt very whole and safe and happy when I was with you. I don't know if I can put aside my emotions for the rest of my life in the service of anthropological objectivity which doesn't seem to me like objectivity at all, but a way of controlling the fear of the foreign.

As you can guess from my tone, I have been feeling quite alienated from my new life. I thought that if I wrote it all down and explained it all to you maybe you could help me see things differently, and maybe, in the process, I'd have a better understanding of what I have gotten myself into.

My dysphoria started with the vest. Do you remember the vest you bought me in Istanbul? It caught my eye as we walked up the main street of the Grand Bazaar on our way to the Sahaflar book market. It was in a pile of vests on the counter of a small stall. At the back of the stall, satin slippers in shimmering colours had been fastened to the fabric covering the wall in orderly rows, and overhead, cotton shirts and tunics in earthy colours were suspended from a horizontal bar. Mounds of sweaters with multi-coloured stripes of thick wool had been placed on every available flat surface.

In that unsettling medley of colours, shapes, and textures, the vest stood out because of its striking colour and the unexpected pattern of its fabric. When I looked at it from the main street, I was sure I had seen blue dragons flying against a crimson sky. Perhaps I was still preoccupied with dragons after hearing you explain the philosophy of Sabbatai Sevi, who had made ample use of metaphors involving dragons. Perhaps the juxtaposition of the cobalt blue pattern on the deep burgundy velvet base attracted my eyes which were still dazzled by the glitter of the gold bracelets and necklaces under the bright yellow spotlights of the display cases we had just passed.

When I brushed my fingers against the fabric, I wondered why I had mistaken the intricate design of paisley, roses, and leaves for flying dragons. You urged me to try it on. I did and immediately liked it. You paid for it without bargaining. I took the vest off because I didn't want to wear it right away. The stall owner took the vest and went to the back of the stall where he kept his wrapping paper. He carefully wrapped it in several layers of white tissue paper before putting it into a green plastic bag advertising his name in large golden letters. As he handed me the bag, I saw him wink at you. You nodded and winked back. Although you had not been overly friendly with each other throughout the transaction, I did not suspect anything when I saw you winking at each other because I assumed that it was normal for Turkish men to use such expressions.

I never wore the vest when I was in Turkey or since I came to Montreal. But this year, in late September, I dug it out from the bottom of the suitcase where I had stored it. When I tried it on, I was shocked to see how loose it was on me. Even when I buttoned it, it was still too baggy. I decided to have it altered.

Costa's tailor shop is on St. Laurent boulevard between Prince Arthur and Pine. Sandwiched between a high-end boutique operated by a French-Canadian gay couple and the post office which is also a stationary store run by Moroccan immigrants, Costa's tailor shop stands as a testament to passive resistance. From the pile of dust on the red nylon ski jacket in the window and the striking degree to which the sign, once boldly black, which declares the "before" and the magical "after" of the grey jacket altered by Costa at least twenty years ago, has yellowed, it is obvious that Costa's display has not been changed in a long, long while.

A wall of smoke hit me as soon as I entered the store. Costa was working in the far corner of the store beyond racks of clothes that are now unsaleable. He was ironing a pair of men's pants with a steam iron, a lit cigarette dangling from his lips. "Where did you get this?" he asked in a thick Portuguese accent, as he pinned my vest along the side seams to make it tighter. His hoarse voice betrayed a long-term nicotine habit. "It reminds me of the fabrics I used to sew when I was a young tailor in Lisbon."

"I bought it in Turkey," I answered.

"It's well made," he commented. "I should have it fixed by Tuesday, but call me first." He handed me his business card with a sewing machine logo printed on the top left corner. It reeked of nicotine and cigarette smoke like everything else in the store.

On the following Tuesday, I went to pick up my vest. Costa had done a good job. I paid him the five dollars I owed him and was about to leave when he peered over his glasses, which were perched low on his thin nose, and said "wait, there was something I wanted to give you. The breast pocket in the lining was sewn up. It was sewn closed by hand, in a fast stitch. I opened it and found a piece of paper there."

Costa reached into the old Tetley tea tin where he kept his stack of business cards. He handed me an unevenly folded note. The paper was faintly lined, unbleached, yellowish, with several small holes in it, like it was torn from a notebook. Written with a lead pencil sharpened by a knife rather than a pencil sharpener, was the following:

"Besami Barohya ile Sabbatay Sevi es Sabbatay Sevi en todos los mondos."

"I couldn't help reading it," he said. "Do you know who Sabbatai Sevi is?"

I nodded.

"He is here in Montreal," said Costa.

I was too flabbergasted to say anything.

"As he is in all the worlds," he added, and winked.

Automatically I winked back because I was nervous.

He beamed with affection as he held my hands in his.

As I walked down St. Laurent and across Prince Arthur towards my home on Terrasse St. Denis I couldn't help wondering if all those who dealt in vests belonged to a secret association with members throughout the world. Were they all in league with Sabbatai Sevi? Who had written the note? How old was it?

I stopped in the middle of Prince Arthur. People were watching me through the window as they ate their blintzes and cabbage soup at the Polish restaurant. I walked a few paces ahead so that I would be out of their sight and pulled out the note from my purse to examine it. Had Costa placed it in my vest? A preposterous thought, but it was possible. Perhaps the fabric and the design of the vest conveyed a special message which had led Costa to scribble the note and give it to me to test me. This was even more improbable. But why then had he asked about the fabric?

My head reeled at the thought that I had crossed the path of the misunderstood messiah once again. I decided not to tell anyone about this, neither David, nor Jacques, not even Professor Klein, my history professor.

They have been looking in again. I have seen them move swiftly across my window. They are furtive, but their breath is heavy. Now that it is colder outside they exhale dense round clouds of breath which remain long after they have scuttled beyond the reach of my stare. When I look up and see scraggly patches of fog outside my window I know they have been looking in. I cannot see the street in front of the house too well because my window is barely higher than street level. I can't focus well anyway if I've been writing or reading for a while. Now that I'm telling you this story, I forget to stare out for long periods of time. This makes it easier for them to watch me. They are attracted to the light in my room. I would be, too, if I lived like them. From the outside, my room must look warm and cozy to them, the yellow light of my desk lamp marking off a spot where thoughts are especially coherent. Being homeless, they exaggerate what those of us with a fixed address have. They value things like desks on which papers remain untouched and lamps whose light bulbs always shine because the burnt-out ones are promptly replaced. I don't have it as good as they think I do here. My thoughts are not always clear. I'm not always happy here, and although I have a roof over my head and a man in the room upstairs I sleep with, I don't feel very secure.

The vagrants watch me because they know that if it weren't for me, David and Jacques would let them in. I'm the one who keeps the door of this sprawling house closed to them, oblivious to their shivering and shuddering in the cold. November tests the kindness of us all. They know that if I'm not letting them in now, I will be merciless by February. Anyone who has spent several winters in a cold place like Montreal knows the winter siege mentality.

The house has started creaking at night. The wooden beams and boards snap and pop through the night like cheap firecrackers good for a half-hearted scare. Every night now, as I lie in my bed and listen to the house crack and groan, I brace myself as I did on all the New Year's Eves of my childhood when a handful of fire-crackers, along with the peremptory smiles on our lips, were expected to ward off the sense of defeat already approaching us from the new year.

I pull my quilt up to my nose, determined to keep the cold and the intruders at bay. I can avoid them only so much because I live with two men who study vagabonds. Jacques says he sees his father in these men, the man who died in a boxing ring in St.

Henri when Jacques was four. I think he sees himself in them. I think if he can understand why they remain homeless, and how they survive on the streets, he would free himself from his fear that he will end up like them because he is fatherless. Some of his friends from the orphanage where he spent his childhood are on the streets now, and he studies them. He says it is easier to have informants who had been your friends and equals at one time. Jacques is studying the life choices available to people who are aging on the street. One choice he believes they should have is to be able to drop in at our apartment at any time.

David, on the other hand, is more of a theoretician. He wonders why urban anthropology is in decline when more people are forced to live in cities with each passing year. He is intrigued by vagrants, vagabonds, and homeless people. He believes that these people are the vanguards of future human networks.

I am terrified that they will bring us diseases. None of us like cleaning the house much. As long as we are the only ones using the toilet, I don't mind sitting on the seat without wiping it first. But the thought of sitting on the toilet after a vagrant has sat there, the thought that I may be drinking from a cup a vagrant has drunk from in my absence and left on the counter, horrifies me. I'm under attack. I'm invaded daily by these men.

Jacques and David tell me I'm overreacting. "How can you be an anthropologist," they ask, "if you can't mask your disgust with the "other"?" They may be right. I may not be cut out to be an anthropologist. I don't believe in associating with people I don't like. I don't feel that I have to like them from the outset just because they belong to the group I study.

The threesome watching me from the street have been inside our house a few times, invited in by Jacques and David. Earlier today David called me into the kitchen as I was on my way to the bathroom to introduce them to me. They have Québécois names:

Ti-Guy, Ti-Jean, and Sage. I hesitated approaching them because they stank. The five men were sitting easily around the kitchen table as though they were old friends finally reunited after years of overseas assignments. I stood beside the table, reluctant to pull up a chair. I was repulsed by the mismatched and smelly rags the three men wore. Legions of germs threatened me silently from the mess of dried vomit, feces and urine lodged in the weft and warp of their pants and jackets. How could I sit at the same table where they rested their filthy arms?

Sage extended a grimy hand to greet me. David was watching me closely. It was a test I had to pass if I hoped to maintain his interest in me. He is so devoted to his work that he'd never tolerate me rejecting his informants. Jacques was amused at my discomfort. He offered me a cigarette which I grabbed, instead of shaking Sage's filthy hand. Undaunted, Sage picked up the lighter from the table and flicked it under my nose. I reached over with the cigarette between my lips to accept his light although I found even the harmless flame repugnant because it came from him. I puffed on the cigarette as if I had a real craving for nicotine. In fact cigarettes make me dizzy. My heart started beating faster, and I thought I'd pass out, but I was proud of my minor victory. I had not been touched by them.

I left the five men in the kitchen and went back to my room. No one will watch me from the window now, because they are sitting in the kitchen. David and Jacques will offer them tea and coffee. As the afternoon progresses Jacques will ask if anyone wants a beer. The vagrants will be polite to the point of shyness. "Whatever you two decide. You are students with schedules. We have no plans," they will say. David will think ahead to what he had planned for the evening. Talking to real informants about their life on the streets instead of reading anthropological theory on urban wanderers will win out. Jacques will run across the street to the depanneur that always smells of insect repellent to buy a case of beer and a large bag of chips, and that's the last I will see of them until David takes out the leftover chicken from the fridge to make chicken sandwiches for everyone. He will yell into the hallway to invite me. I will stand in the hallway, wave at them in the kitchen and say I've eaten. It is not a lie because I will have gone to the health food store at the corner of Sherbrooke and St. Denis to buy humus and a loaf of whole wheat bread and eaten it upstairs in the living room, away from their stench and the garbled conversations in broken English and French.

When I think of studying vagrants, or nomads, or whatever anyone wants to call them, I think of studying clean people who bathe in the desert sun, completing their ablutions with fistfuls of desert sand. I think of self-sufficient, secretive people who'd rather breathe the air of freedom and be poor than work to someone else's rules. Where do such nomads live? Do they belong only to the past and the pages of historical novels? Because the anthropologists I have met here don't know where they are, either.

On the first day of classes four years ago the department chairman asked to see me. He is a stocky American who wears an African turtle ring which has stained his ring finger permanently green. He asked me what I intended to write my Ph.D. thesis on. I wasn't quite sure. My first impulse was to run away from him and the department.

"Gypsies," I blurted.

"We don't have gypsies in Canada," he responded.

I waited awhile, hoping he would remember that bands of North American gypsies make a pilgrimage to Ste. Anne, Quebec, every year. I was going to suggest that the pilgrimage site could be a starting point for my research. He didn't remember anything about gypsies and I let the subject drop because I didn't want to risk correcting the department chairman during our initial meeting.

"How about vagabonds, then?" I ventured, "you know, people on the move."

"We call them nomads in this department," he said with utmost seriousness.

"Nomads?"

He seemed pleased. "The nomad specialist in our department is Professor Stillman. He is anxious to meet you. He is the one who really wanted you in this department, by the way."

I spent the first year trying to avoid Professor Stillman. He had been kicked out of Iran by Khomeini for staring at the nomads, but staring is a prized activity among anthropologists. They call it "participant observation," an oxymoron if there ever was one. Professor Stillman is always watching the main hallway in the anthropology department through his office door, which he always leaves half open. During the entire first year when he saw me walking down the hallway, he would thrust his bald head out and try to lure me into his rug-lined office with cloying promises of freshly brewed tea, like a shopkeeper at the Grand Bazaar. I would acquiesce because I was a newcomer to the department and I hadn't learned yet how to turn down the false hospitality of anthropologists.

I still don't know how to deal with them. After nearly four years, Professor Stillman still thinks I'll go along with his plans and return to Turkey to study nomads in the Taurus mountains once I pass my comprehensive exams. He assures me they are just as interesting as the nomads he was studying in Iran. He hints at a collaboration on a comparative article he has been asked to write on Middle Eastern and Balkan nomads for the *American*

Anthropologist. I don't have the courage to explain myself. I delay the inevitable by pretending I'm too busy writing my Ph.D. proposal. How can I tell him I'm not interested in spending my life staring at people?

I realize that if I want to survive among anthropologists I have to become like them. I have to learn how to watch the world and be uninvolved with it. Believe me, I have tried, but I got sick in the process.

Do you remember Ali, when you wanted to show me the synagogue on a side street below the Galata tower, they wouldn't let us in because I said I was an American but I didn't have my passport on me, and you said you were a tourist guide but you didn't have your license on you. The synagogue guard was suspicious. You had been inside many times before, but you wanted to show me the most popular synagogue in Istanbul. You persuaded the guard to plead your case to the management and left me waiting on the street for you.

It was a narrow, cobble-stoned street with all kinds of shops beneath the apartment buildings. On the sidewalk a vendor was selling plastic hair trinkets and airmail envelopes. The traffic squeezed through the narrow passage between the rows of cars parked bumper to bumper on both sides of the street. It was a sunny day. I didn't see the boy or his bear approach me. A bear cub is smaller than a European car. I didn't hear the jingle of the bell hanging from a rope collar around the bear's neck. Softly, they came, sure of their footing on that crowded street as they would have been on a wide open field. The boy was probably no older than ten, but he had the wizened face of an adult gypsy who has been making a living on the streets ever since he could walk on his own behind a bear.

The boy put his arm on the bear's shoulder and the bear

balanced himself on its two hind legs with the aid of a walking stick the boy placed under his front left paw and they both rested in front of the steel door of the synagogue.

"One dollar," said the boy.

"One dollar for what?" I asked.

"One dollar to take photo," he said.

"I don't want to take a photo," I answered.

"One dollar. This is good bear," he emphasized.

I smiled, but I didn't respond.

"Where you come from?" he asked.

"United States," I answered.

"California? Miami?"

"No, New York," I replied.

"Bear like this in New York?"

"No," I said.

"One dollar for picture," he insisted.

"All right," I said, and took a photo of the gypsy boy grinning widely with his serious bear leaning on a walking stick in front of the steel synagogue door that was bolted to iron hoops set in concrete blocks on the street.

I gave the boy an extra dollar. "For the bear," I said.

They disappeared behind a van that was parked a few paces ahead, and that was the last I saw of them.

You returned soon after and told me they wouldn't let us into the synagogue unless we had proper identification. I lamented that there were no windows through which we could peek to see the interior of the synagogue without having to go in. You said that most synagogues were shut off from the world because of the fear that Jewish people had of being attacked. I said, "Windows and doors give access both ways. This is also how they keep themselves separate from the rest of the world." You commented that I was beginning to sound like you. All I wanted was to see the inside of that synagogue, to satisfy my curiosity and to soak up the energy of their prayers, but I wasn't permitted to because I couldn't prove my identity to the guard.

Tonight I took out the photo of the gypsy boy and several other photos from Istanbul which you never saw because I had my films from the trip developed after I came to Montreal. I spread the photos on my bed. I have been looking at them. The gypsy boy is the kind of vagabond I could follow. I hear David, Jacques, and the three dirty men laughing in the kitchen.

I must have drifted into sleep looking at the photo of the gypsy boy and the bear in front of the synagogue in Istanbul because I woke up in the middle of the night, shivering and thirsty. The photograph of the bear was crumpled under my arm. The first thing I saw when I opened my eyes was the bear staring at me.

I got up from the bed, put away the photos that were scattered on the Guatemalan blanket that Jacques has lent me, and changed into my nightgown. I went to the bathroom, drank a glass of milk in the kitchen, trying to keep away from the mess left behind by the vagrants and my housemates, and then came back and got under the covers. I couldn't fall back to sleep.

I felt as if I'd been carrying a heavy load on my back all night. A tall load with sharp edges. Then I remembered the dream I must have been dreaming before I woke up. In the dream I was a bearer of spiritual books. Books and porters and travelers started me thinking of you again, Ali, so I lay in my bed remembering your house in Buyukada, the nights we spent in that magical house together under the peach colored satin quilt, the howl of the wind blowing in from the Marmara sea, the pomegranate tree whose branches tapped the small window in the cubbyhole off the kitchen that was our bedroom, and of course, your body, your warmth against my body.

I have never been able to feel completely at ease with anyone, Ali. No man has ever been able to enter that soft shell of light that accompanies me everywhere I go. But with you, I wasn't trying. I felt as if our solitudes were in accord, that neither of us had invaded the other, that we were ready to offer each other a collection of keys, some good, some old and ornamental, some functional to be used to understand each other. I was hesitant to remain with you in your space. I enjoyed it, but I felt that I had other things to accomplish, more important things on this side of the ocean.

Why, I wonder, did I mention keys when you gave me a ring which has been of great help to me. I turn it around on my finger a few times every time I want to clear my thoughts. The "S" carved into the carnelian stone sometimes looks like the serpent of eternity to me, and sometimes like a wave or a sand dune, but it works every time. My mind always clears. At the very least I'm on my own, removed from whatever is bothering me. It is a magical ring, a healing ring as you said it was, and I'm grateful to you for it.

I really wonder about my decision to come to Montreal. I am studying things at McGill that have no relevance to the world as I have experienced it with you or on my own. I am sleeping with a man who treats me like a stranger the next day; whose mother considers me to be a threat to her well-being and to their family line, and by extension, a menace to the continuity of Jews in the world because I'm a shiksa!

I met David and Jacques on the first day of classes, the same day I met the department chairman and Professor Stillman. That afternoon there was an orientation party in the lounge of the anthropology department. David and Jacques were standing in front of the refreshments table drinking wine, when I reluctantly joined the party. They introduced themselves to me as I poured myself a glass of Pepsi.

Jacques, in his jovial French-Canadian way, joked about the drinking habits of the professors, making me feel at ease, while David asked about my academic plans. He seemed very interested in what I had done at Yale. When I told him about my conversation with the department chairman, he warned me against Professor Stillman who, he said, had a habit of imposing himself on the fresh female recruits. I responded that judging by the number of females present at the party, Professor Stillman must have been very busy the last few years. Besides David and Jacques, I noted only four other male graduate students at the gathering. Females, on the other hand, numbered over thirty. I admit I enjoyed the precious male attention. Afterwards, Jacques asked me if I would like to come over for dinner. When I hesitated David insisted that I accept. That's when I realized that these two were housemates.

That evening they asked me to move in with them. Since the house was so big and quaint, and I was comfortable with them, and the room that was to be mine, which is the room I am writing to you from now, seemed so ideal for studying, and the rent was so attractive compared to the bachelor apartment unit I had rented in the McGill student ghetto, I agreed to live with them. I moved in within a week of subletting my own apartment.

Initially Jacques was the one who flirted with me, finding opportunities for us to do things together without David. But I was attracted to David's studiousness, his sense of purpose, his quiet and reflective moods. I was also attracted to his Jewishness, which manifested itself in the sureness with which David handled everyday events. Having grown up without much parental guidance or support, mostly in boarding schools, I am awed by people who exhibit a sense of assurance about the mundane.

What I didn't realize at first was David's unusual attachment to his mother. Although he appeared to be independent, living apart from her, spending time with non-Jews, and doing field-work with the kinds of people she would never admit into her own home, he was, in fact, strongly influenced by her. Slowly, because with David, everything involving emotions is very slow, he acknowledged that he cannot conceive of ever contradicting his mother or standing up for something she does not approve of because he doesn't want to hurt her.

Both of David's brothers have left town. One lives in Toronto, and the other in New Jersey. David, the eldest, cannot leave her. Sometimes I think that even as an anthropologist he will not venture far. He will study urban wanderers as long as they wander around Montreal.

For over a year David did not tell his mother that we had a relationship. I wonder what he has told her in the last four years, because he has admitted to me that since I'm not Jewish, it would break his mother's heart if he told her he loves me. I don't think he wants to love me. We still sleep in separate beds. At first David said it was best if we kept our relationship secret from Jacques. Then he didn't want his mother to know. Of course he also didn't want the department to know. Slowly they all learned about us, but our sleeping arrangement hasn't changed. I think David would feel as if he were betraying his mother if we joined our beds.

Whatever she thinks of me and my relationship with her son, David's mother talks to me several times a day! A typical conver-sation between us goes like this:

"Helloo, how are you?" she asks hurriedly, as if she hasn't

spoken to me in a long time and she is genuinely happy to find me on the other end of the phone.

I take a deep breath. I will not be annoyed. She is David's mother and I want to keep the peace with her.

"How are you today?"

She has called earlier at lunchtime and asked this already. She has also found out what I had for lunch and what David brought with him to eat at McGill. She has neither approved not criticized. Now she will want to know what's for supper.

"What are you having for dinner?"

I try to sound calm. "We haven't decided yet." I'm waiting for David to come home.

"He's always late, isn't he?"

"No, not always, he has a late class today."

"You don't take the same classes?"

"No we don't." She knows this already. We study different things. We have told her, but she will ask again.

"It's not too late to have dinner?"

"It's alright. I had a snack already."

"David must be famished."

"I'm sure he can eat something if he is really hungry."

"He's lost weight," she says, with an edge of brittle disapproval in her voice, meaning "you are starving my son."

"He swims almost every day. He's actually healthier."

"Make sure he doesn't get too tired."

"I'll try," I say civilly. "And how are you?"

"Considering the weather, I guess I'm all right."

"How is your arthritis today?" I've asked this question already today, but this is a question I can't go wrong with. Mrs. Lerner loves talking about her arthritis.

"I had a bit of trouble opening a can of soup tonight, but other than that I guess I'm all right."

What does she want? How can we alleviate her misery? Should I die so she can have her son back so that she never has to open another can again?

"They said on the radio it's supposed to rain tonight. Have you had rain there, yet?"

It's an absurd question. How can the climate differ between where she lives in Côte St. Luc and where we live on St. Denis? But for Mrs. Lerner this is a weird world where rain can fall in one part of the city and bypass another, yes, a very strange and unfair world where good Jewish boys like her son are snatched by scheming shiksas like myself.

"No we haven't, Mrs. Lerner," I say. "But it looks like rain. It's quite humid."

She manages to sound bored as well as defeated when she finally says in her fragile voice, "Well, I won't keep you longer dear, you must be busy."

"It's all right."

"Will you tell David I called?"

Of course I will. I will tell David, but he won't call her back because he doesn't know what to say to her. He won't tell her that he is frustrated with her. She won't mention to him that she called tonight even though she knew he wouldn't be here when she called. She will blame me for keeping her son away from her, but she will never openly say it. There is no winning in all of this for any of us, least of all me, because I'm the evil shiksa who has stolen a good Jewish boy away from his widowed mother who has sacrificed her whole life for her sons only to be abandoned by them in her old age.

It actually sounds funny and much less painful now that I've written this down. I really have to do something about these calls. I have gone to see a hypnotherapist, Onno Van Loon, a Dutchman who has been living in Montreal for a while. He can induce a trance in either English or French. I had been having odd nightmares lately and muscle pains which exhaust me. I feel old and tired in this city, burdened by a history that isn't mine. Then I wonder if it is my history after all, because I believe that time is not linear. It is quite possible that we have lived several lifetimes with the same intentions and the same dreams; and that each moment of the present engenders many other presents, pasts, and futures, and that some of us, like myself and you, travel among them more consciously than others. We may be able to take pieces of lives from different realities and graft them on to each other. Therefore, what ends up puzzling us about the nature of reality is what we have done to it, ourselves!

David thinks hypnotherapy is not a real therapy. He concedes it has entertainment value and an anthropological interest value as a primitive religious practice which has evolved into a form acceptable to the contemporary western world. He doesn't see hypnotherapy as a spiritual learning process as I do, a viable method for increased self awareness and a means for altering unwanted behaviour patterns. When I point out that my muscle pains have decreased, that I have fewer nightmares, and less anxiety about my life, he says I could have had the same results with a bottle of aspirin, a box of mint tea, and a good appointment book. Jacques wonders if I'd be able to resist Onno if he made sexual advances while I was under his influence!

It's been two weeks since I last wrote this letter. One of these days I'll finish it and, maybe, even mail it to you.

I've been attending a class on the history of European Jewry at McGill, partly because I'm intrigued by old books and foreign cultures, and partly to comprehend the source of David's mother's animosity toward me. How could a grown woman accuse her own son and her son's girlfriend of sabotaging the survival of the Jews? She considers him a traitor to his own people because he is sleeping with a non-Jew; while she treats him as if he were the messiah who has all the power in the world to single-handedly deliver the Jews to their promised glory! I'm beginning to think David is no saner than his mother is because he cannot bring himself to challenge her. He must believe that there is some truth to her irrational convictions. As Jacques quipped to me once, "Too bad, Mr. Lerner had to die before he could invent the zipper that would close his wife's mouth." (Mr. Lerner made his million manufacturing zippers. He sold them all over Canada and the USA. He died around the same time velcro strips were gaining a share of the market that had been exclusively his.)

Everybody talks except me. I listen, I think, I turn my thoughts over and over in my head. Onno, my hypnotherapist, thinks it's time I voiced what's on my mind. I don't know. Maybe this letter is the beginning of all that has been quietly churning inside of me. It is as if my tongue has been suppressed, like a sharp knife kept in a sheath, and I'm afraid to draw it out and discover that it will cut everything it touches. Or, that it wasn't too sharp to start with, so why did I keep it stored for so long—a last resort?

Last week, Professor Klein taught a class on Sabbatai Sevi. He started the lecture by saying that he was criticized by his colleagues for refusing to call him a false messiah. He said Sabbatai Sevi's message should not be dismissed, however blasphemous it seems. "If we call him false from the start, we will not be able to discuss his teachings with an open mind," he said, "and that is against the Jewish tradition of debate." A few of the students in class, those who wear skullcaps all the time, protested fervently.

Two young men who always sit at the front row commented that if this is the kind of history Professor Klein was going to teach, they might as well drop his course.

In his time Sabbatai Sevi reached a cross-cultural audience. This is what impresses me most. He not only attracted Christian followers, but also Muslim followers. In fact, his followers, if they exist at all in the present, are found among secular Muslims in Istanbul, Izmir, and the Balkans. They are so secretive that they only inform their children of their true religious identity when the children are well into adulthood. Some members of these families never learn who they really are. Sabbatai Sevi believed that the Jewish soul must pass through all the world religions before it can gather the broken pieces of light (the shekhinah) which are scattered around the world. These scattered pieces are concentrated mostly among the Muslims, he said. Therefore, a Jew must be a Muslim before he can truly become a Jew! (I'm not sure if Mrs. Lerner could follow this argument.)

Professor Klein said that those who still practice the Sabbatean principles are known as "donmes" or "turners." They probably live in Istanbul. Which then got me thinking about you, Ali. For a while, sitting in the class, I was convinced that I had finally found the secret tribe that all anthropologists dream of discovering one day, and that you were the leader of the tribe. Not only that, but I had found the source of the wisdom that counsels the world's most intransigent people to turn into something else before they can be healed. Sabbatai Sevi declared that the truest acts of redemption are those which cause the greatest scandals at any given time in history. Since marranos of any religion, those who profess to believe in one religion, but secretly practice another, have always caused the biggest scandals in history, they must be the true carriers of God's message. "Does this mean that everyone must, in some way, share the fate of marranos, before the world can be healed, and the shekhinah can overcome the darkness?" asked Professor Klein. The orthodox Jews in the class groaned when he asked us to write a short essay on this question for the following class.

Professor Klein went on to say that there were almost no original written sources to illustrate the Sabbatean philosophy. He showed us a few slides of broadsheets from the seventeenth century which were fictional depictions of the apostasy of Sabbatai Sevi. The only autographed letter by Sabbatai Sevi is a document in Hebrew in which he asks the Albanian Jewish community for a prayer book for the High Holidays, and this, after he became a Muslim!

As I sat in class it occurred to me that perhaps the collected works of the Sabbateans have never been revealed to the world because the world is still not ready for their truth. The crisis of Sabbateanism occurred in 1666. If you invert the numerals, you get 1999. Perhaps that is when the Sabbatean teachings will come to light. I'm afraid to discuss these thoughts with anyone else but you, Ali, because they might think I've gone completely insane. The mental health clinic is conveniently located up the street from the Jewish Studies building. They'd direct me there if I shared these thoughts with them.

> lit up high mountains
> darkness was here no longer
> —had not come from holy places—
> redeemer showed the way the Torah
> lit up high mountains
> was born the sun that heals
> healed the Shekinah
> her wisdom came on us
> lit up high mountains

he MY REMEMBRANCE says I'm faithful
to believers in Zevi Sultan
my belief in him a tree
lit up high mountains
days since he crushed that snake
lit up high mountains
lit up the moon by daylight

This is the poem that Professor Klein handed out at the end of the class. He suggested that it might become a research topic for some of us for the final essay. "Think of the possibility that Sara, the prostitute and convert wife of Sabbatai Sevi, was the personification of the shekhinah," he said. The orthodox Jewish students I told you about scoffed and left the room in a huff. I lingered behind and waited until the rest of the students had left.

"Professor Klein," I said. A nervous man in ordinary circumstances, this class had taken its toll on him. His hands shook as he collected the papers on his desk. He tried to smile. "Yes?"

"I might be able to locate original Sabbatean documents." I immediately regretted saying this, but I couldn't take it back. It had been uttered.

He raised his eyebrows. "Where?"

"Not here. In Istanbul."

"If you found even half a prayer your contribution to world scholarship would be immense," he said.

"May I consult you on the authenticity if I'm able to secure a document?"

He was shaking visibly. He lowered his head and took a deep breath. "You will find a true friend in me, Sara," he answered, conspiratorially.

I hadn't expected to hear such an emotional response from

him. Because he was always so aloof during class, so insistent about being objective and professorial in all his interactions, I had assumed that he would always keep a barrier between himself and a student. I didn't follow him into the hall. Now, I can't help wondering if Professor Klein is also a Sabbatean. Is this why he refuses to call Sabbatai Sevi a false messiah?

I don't want to discuss this topic any further with him. I am really afraid of appearing paranoid or delusional. I am also afraid of becoming involved in something very bizarre if this secret organization really exists. I need you to help me out, Ali. I will not mention the documents or your library to anyone until you write back to me.

It was a day of revelations. After class, I went for a cup of coffee and carrot cake at the Shangri-La Café at Peel and Sherbrooke. I sat at a table by the window, watching the traffic on Sherbrooke street and the people at the bus stop in front of the café. The end of the work day is the best time for watching people on that corner. All the office buildings empty out at that hour and conservatively dressed people fill the street with that inscrutable sense of propriety that mainstream Canadians have even after a long and tiring workday. I watched them crowd the street and be whisked away by the buses that came and went in quick succession. Soon, the dark street was empty of traffic. Relief. Downtown was mine again.

This is the time I like to visit the library, when it feels like a huge ship floating on the calm sea that is a long fall evening in Canada. Its ancient cargo gives me a sense of security and reassurance. I feel that I belong to downtown Montreal and its cosmopolitan anguish when I'm in the library in the evening.

After doing some preliminary research on the computer, I went upstairs to the Jewish history section. Among books on the

Holocaust and the Talmud, Spinoza and Israel, I was shocked to find a book on Rembrandt. The large square-shaped book was titled, appropriately, *The Jews in the Age of Rembrandt*. Its cover showed a greatly enlarged detail from a small Rembrandt print which was originally 3x5 inches.

I held the book, transfixed by the two old men in oriental kaftans and headgear to the right of the cover, wondering where I had seen men like this before. I remembered all those drawings and engravings of Ottomans which I had seen in the museums of Istanbul and of course, the photographs you showed me of your family. I was especially reminded of a photograph from the end of the 19th century of a Jewish merchant who, you said, spent his summers in your house in Buyukada. I was struck by the similarities of their round bushy beards and the long kaftans that fell to their ankles. The merchant in the photograph on your living room wall must have been wealthier than the men in Rembrandt's print because I remember that his kaftan was better fitted, and tufts of fur, perhaps only rabbit fur, but fur nevertheless, protruded from the front of it.

The men in Rembrandt's engraving and in the photographs at your house all wore similar types of shoes and socks. Their socks were thick and sturdy, almost like gaiters inside the leather shoes that were molded around their feet. They all looked ready to walk, if necessary, over mountains and across valleys. I was wondering why most of the Jews in old drawings and etchings were depicted as if they were ready to move on, when I noticed the man to the left of the book cover whose body was cut in half by the book's spine.

He was sitting on a slab of stone, his back to everyone else and the synagogue door, his thumb in his mouth, looking totally ambivalent about whether to stay or to go. That man was certainly a sitter, not a walker; a thinker, not a talker. I turned the book over to look at his back, but the book's spine had consumed most of his back in the binding. To the left of the back cover were two men, again, deep in conversation, bent conspiratorially toward each other. The sitter, the lonely one, had been excised from Jewish history although he formed its spine. I was thinking of who he had been in real life when Rembrandt sketched him, and how he looked familiar because I identified with him when I realized I had seen him before.

Wasn't he on the wall of the cubby hole in Buyukada where you kept your bed? I remember falling asleep there, with the moon-light streaming in through the window and lighting up that small yellowed print in its cracked wooden frame. I remember thinking over and over again, before I fell asleep, who was that man, who was that man, although you told me it was Salih Effendi, the friend of your ancestral namesake, Ali Effendi. I did not believe you when you told me the print was probably a Rembrandt original. I simply could not believe that someone in Istanbul could have a Rembrandt original. I am convinced now of the truth. The truth, although strange and twisted and oh, so foggy, is out there, and you are out there, Ali, and perhaps you are the messiah!

For sure, you are my messiah. You should come here. You must come here to the West and heal me. I am lost at the end of the second millennium here. I don't know where to turn. The people here have no knowledge of history or the efforts of those before us who have traveled the earth in search of truth and God. You were patiently waiting, and I finally understood, as I stood that Friday night in the library with the book in my hand, its plastic coated cover slippery in my sweaty palms, that I had finally found you, my messiah, my beloved, that I would support you and follow you, introduce you to the West and translate for you. I promise to be your scribe and your wife, the singer of your songs, the repeater of your riddles. But come here, please come here, because the emptiness here in the West, here in my heart needs to be filled by a model of a man, a model worthy of a Rembrandt.

SIX

Her Last Session

SARA LAY on a blue mat in the hypnotherapist's office in downtown Montreal. She had entered a deep trance state within minutes of commencing the session. Although her body remained inert on the mat, she responded alertly to Onno's questions as a rapid sequence of sensations flooded her consciousness.

"I feel a bird coming over, a big black bird with very large wings."

"How do you feel when you see this bird?"

"Strength. Big bird. Big black bird. It's flying in circles over me. People believe in the bird."

"Is there power in the bird?"

"A lot of power."

"Tell me about the power of the bird."

"This bird is able to see everything. Past and future. It can go to the lands where the white people are and come back with stories. I'm good with the bird. I'm very good with the bird. Actually, I trained the bird. I feed the bird, I keep the bird."

"He is your friend."

"Yeah, I have powers. I have lots of powers. If I want to I can heal, if I want to I can put a curse. I can do many things, but I don't do those things."

"Why not?"

"Because I don't want to hurt people."

"You've got the power to hurt?"

"Yeah. Oh, I can hurt if I want to."

"But you have the power to love."

"Yeah, but I'm really alone. There's a girl I really like. I have to be alone with this, I have to be alone with this. We're supposed to be single."

"Why is that?"

"We're supposed to be single; we've always been single."

"Do they know you have these powers?"

"Yeah, and they respect me for it. I love her so much."

"Does she feel that?"

"I don't know her very much. She knows that I'm a human being. I'm always alone; I'm with people, but I'm always alone."

"How do you project fear?"

"Fear?"

"Why do people fear you?"

(Sigh) "There's something lacking in me."

"Is it lacking, or are you afraid to express it?"

"Maybe I'm afraid to express it."

"So what happened with these birds and the girl?"

(Sniff) "I had a beautiful body. And it was very sunny the whole time. I was a diviner and a healer. I see some snakes, too. Yeah, I could live with snakes, too."

"You like to touch them?"

"Hmmm, not really, but I don't mind them, you know."

"Do they come to you?"

"Uhuh. They like me, they like me a lot. Snakes, reptiles, salamanders, they like me. That's one reason why the people fear me, because I'm good with them. Spiders, strange animals, they like me, and I let them be. I lived for a very long time, to a very old age."

"Alone all the time?"

"With a lot of animals."

"Never went after a woman?"

"I wanted to."

"Why did you stop yourself?"

"Because of my powers."

"Why did your powers restrict you?"

"Because you have to keep them strong."

"Why is that?"

"I don't know. It's the way it's always been; something to do with the power's involvement. They don't want us to share it with humans, and I'm in between. I loved her so much."

"You were afraid to show your love?"

"She knew, but she couldn't wait very long. She had beautiful black curls, beautiful black curls. I don't know where I am. Is this Syria maybe, or Egypt or Irak? I think it's someplace like that; Palestine maybe? Yeah, I think it's Palestine. (Sniff) She was beautiful."

"Did you meet her often?"

"Yeah, I'd see her. She used to bring me water, food. I would have liked to have been a father, have children by her, but I couldn't because I wasn't allowed. I had contact with some people, (laughing, in a louder voice) extraterrestials or something."

"Tell me about them."

"They're like… white people, and they're so full of light."

"How do you feel in their presence?"

"Ahh, I feel happy; I feel so happy and light. They're really light people; light, light, very light; they're always with me."

"There are many of them?"

"Uhuh."

"Can you count them?"

"Maybe...Well, the ones that come to see me, they're about five or six of them."

"Did they have different names, did they have names?"

"Yeah, they're strange names, though. Something with "v", Vashyash, I think. They're so, they're light."

"Can other people see them?"

"No."

"Only for you."

"Yeah, but they tell me things."

"Tell me about the things they tell you."

"I'm a messenger, I'm an ally for them."

"Keep on."

"It's about the earth and water."

"What do they say about the world?"

"There is water in a cup, in a bowl, and the thing about water is that it takes the shape of what it's put into, and somehow I'm like that."

"What do you mean?"

"I take the shape of what I'm put into."

"Repeat."

"I have to take the shape of what I'm put into. I'm put into this shape for a reason. It's my reason, I can't forget it. Aahh, I can't forget it, I can't forget it; so much light, so much light." (Starts singing in a barely audible voice)

"Repeat this."

"They'll never let me forget it, they'll never let me forget it."

"So you have to take the shape..."

"Of what I'm put into. I see something like a peacock's feather, and something like a cross, except that it's not a cross, it's like a bowl, and then like a tulip, and like a stem and like a cross like this." (Motioning)

"Do you like the sight of this?"

"Yeah, very much."

"What does it do to you?"

"It's light."

"Can you feel it in your body? Does it have an effect on you?"

(Sigh) "It's like my essence, my essence, and when I see that, I feel light, a white light. They're so beautiful, you can't imagine; when they appear to me, they're so beautiful."

"Tell me how they're beautiful."

"They're so light, they're like crystal, and blue, and everything in them is light. You can see through them, and yet they're real, and it doesn't matter they don't have the same bodies, it doesn't matter all. I'm never alone because of them, I'm never, ever alone. They'll be with me all the time. I will always be protected. Always be protected. There's a door, I see a door. Yeah, I must have gone through that door, on this side..." (Sigh)

"Why can't you get in?"

"I was sent, I was sent over ......" (Long silence followed by sniffing several times)

"... My nose is bleeding, I think I got hit by a stone, I got hit by a stone." (Sniffing through a blocked nose)

"Who threw the stone?"

"I don't know who threw the stone. (sniff) My nose is bleeding, there is a big pool of blood, big pool of blood by the side of the road."

"Tell me what happened."

"I was walking on the road, there was a canal by the road, there were some trees, and I was thinking, I was thinking maybe I have to leave." (Sigh)

"Why do you have to leave?"

(Inhaling through a blocked nose) "Well, it's getting tense

here because it's not peaceful anymore." (Sniff)

"Why did they throw stones at you?"

"They suspect me."

"You're suspected of what?"

"Heresy, heresy. They think I'm causing something, some deaths, diseases or something; they think their problems are because of me. I can't keep up the façade anymore. I don't believe in the same things they do. They think I do magic." (Screaming with pain) "Oohh, my body hurts; (screaming) ohh, they're torturing me, ahh, ahh, they're trying to torture me."

"Did they tie you up?"

"Ah yes;" (sounds of tossing and thrashing) "they're trying to break me, break me."

"What do they say while they're doing that?"

"Ahhh, confess! Confess! Confess! I say there's nothing to confess. There's nothing to confess. They push it, they push it some more. My body, my body. They're breaking my bones, they're making my body longer."

"Show me how."

"Pulling me, pulling it like this."

"Pull pull, stretch it."

(Screaming and crying) "Aah, they're tearing it apart."

"Stretch it!"

"Aaaah." (long screams) "Aah." (gasping for air) "I'm torn."

"Don't move, just do that."

"I'm torn, hmmhmhm."

"Tell me what you hear."

(Long pause followed by a flat, different voice) "He's dead. He'll die rather than sign it."

(Previous voice) "I don't want to be a Catholic, I don't want to be a Catholic. I've got so much pain in my body. I didn't sign it." (Whispers the same sentence several times)

"You didn't sign it. Are you happy you didn't sign it?"

(Nods)

"Show me how happy."

"I'm torn, but I'm not Catholic." (Hysterical, loud laughter of victory) "Hahhahah. I fooled them. They thought they'd get me. Ahh, oh, no, I won't sign their little stupid paper. Oh no I wouldn't. I didn't sign it. Hehehehe, hahahah, I had all these books. Anyway, they can't read Hebrew. Heheheh. Aahh, there's a woman. I don't know if she is my wife or I'm her. Hahahah, ah, I have so many books."

"Repeat that."

"I have so many books, so many books. Hahahah, I'll always have books. Hahaha, I know more languages than they can even count. I write forwards and backwards, and up and down. Hahaha, I write with red ink and black ink, blue ink and green ink, and yellow ink and invisible ink. I have so many books."

"You have so many faces."

"Yeehh." (Laughing nonstop, victoriously) "I can change. Ah boy, I can be so old, middle-aged, and sometimes I'm a woman, ah fuck it, one thing I can't be is a little kid."

"Repeat it."

"One thing I can't be is a little kid." (Sadly repeats the phrase) "It's not safe to be a child."

"Why not?"

(Long silence) "Because it took me so long to come here."

"Where are you?"

(In a calmer voice) "I'm surrounded by books. The air is sweet. I feel the sun on my face. I'm sitting cross-legged on a counter. There are books around me."

"Are there other people?"

"Yes, they come to look at my books. These people are my

friends. They have large white hats made of scarves wound around their heads. Some of them buy my books. I'm drinking tea. My fingers burn when I hold the glass teacup, but I like this. The people ask me questions about my books. I know all the answers."

"Are you a scholar or a bookseller?"

"I'm both. It was a long time ago. I am finally happy. I am a grown man, but I have the heart of a child. I hear something strange, a long song."

"Listen to the words. What do the words say?"

"The song is inviting people to pray. It is in a foreign language. I learned it when I came here."

"Do you go after the song?"

"I stay with my books. There are prayers inside my books that are secrets. I have to wait."

"Haven't you waited enough?"

(Silence.) (Slowly, with deliberation) "I am told I must wait some more. The prayers will be heard when people are ready to change without fear."

"And if your life isn't long enough?"

"Ahh, this is sad. I will pass them on. The prayer will always have new guardians …"

"How do you feel?"

"Strange."

"Open your eyes. Now Sara."

"I remember everything, it's amazing. Some of this stuff I think I had dreams about."

"The dream you had last night of the old house and the robbers is exactly all this."

"It's all so strange. That was quite a stretch on the rack."

"How do you feel about it?"

"Who are these white people? They're like extraterrestrials."

"Well, whatever they are, whatever you saw, the main thing is that it does something to cure you."

"This image you mean?"

"All these images you see. You should listen to this tape carefully, and instead of thinking that what you saw is reality..."

"Yeah?"

"See it through the reality you're living on a day to day basis, and they all have their place, and all your personalities are involved in there. It is all you, but in symbols. If you look at those people as real people you will keep wondering about your life for a long time. You see, when we're born we're the light, that's what we are. We come from an explosion, from the big explosion that started the universe, the big bang: we come from that. So every time we give life, we produce the same explosion; that's the way life came, and through that explosion, there's light. So there's air involved, there's movement involved, there's matter involved. So it's all there. So what you saw is what we remember somewhere in our conscious mind of what happened because we have all the knowledge of this from the beginning. So we are memory. Actually, you're going through your memory, but the unconscious talks to us in symbolic ways. It's not bad, or good, it just is. Period. And through symbols the unconscious is telling you where you are now. The unconscious is creating the equilibrium in the neuroses that you suffer. But there's not going to be as much tension any more. Your dreams are going to change. Write them down if you can."

"I always do."

"And be aware of the messages you receive. Like books, like you have many books, but there is a lot you didn't say, that you have to say. It has to be said in order to be clear, and you're afraid to say it because they involve rage and anger."

"And heresy."

"Well, heresy comes from the fact that the people around you twist the truth and you tell the truth. It's like the truth must prevail. You're telling the truth, but you're always told you're lying. It's like you're in another world. You're with all these people who look like you, who were rejected; but it doesn't come, I think, from past life."

"No?"

"From now."

"So what I experienced were not past lives then?"

"I don't want to break your dream, but how old are you?"

"Twenty-eight."

"Twenty-eight. Maybe it's time for you to wake up. You have those powers that you're talking about. They're real, I've seen them today. You have the power to go inside to change. Either you do or you don't. It's your choice. We're born free. Your unconscious told you where they are. It told you through birds, and snakes, and reptiles...."

As Onno went on, trying to convince Sara that what she had just experienced were mere symbols and metaphors, Sara sat in the armchair across from him, twirling the ring on the ring finger of her right hand. Between her left thumb and index finger, her ring turned; the large S carved into the carnelian stone at its centre gave way to the vine which traversed its flat silver band. She continued turning the ring. Once again, the stone. Once again, the circle was completed.

She often played with her ring when she wanted an answer to a question. When she was in Istanbul she had watched gypsy fortune tellers peer at the configuration of ashes on the surface of a bowl of water, or examine the chance arrangement of a fistful of dried beans on an handkerchief to catch a glimpse of the past and the future. She felt that her ring gave her the same power and the same clarity of mind when she twirled it.

No, she wasn't convinced at all that the people she had sensed in her body during the previous hypnosis session were mere metaphors. Onno was wrong. Somehow, she had been these people, they had been her in the past, and her present embodied their dreams and hopes and frustrations from the past. She, Sara, was the man on the rack and the man sitting in the midst of his books. She was the diviner who was in contact with the light beings who were angelic extraterrestrials, as well the woman who he had loved, but was not allowed to touch. If she could understand her past lives, she would be able to rearrange her present and future lives into a happier, more unified whole. If she could reach her past she would rescue her future.

"It is all a matter of vision isn't it, Onno?"

"No," he replied firmly. "It is all about pent-up anger."

"So that's what you think is wrong with me, that I cannot express my anger?"

"Yes. You and my other client who is also studying anthropology both have difficulty expressing your anger."

"I thought I expressed it plenty. Especially today. I screamed a lot and I cried. I'm exhausted. You don't think that was anger?"

"In a way, yes," Onno assented, "but all those emotions were not directed at the cause of your anger. Your real test will be in the real world, when you can confront the people who have harmed you."

"I don't feel as if they've harmed me."

"They have made you uncomfortable in your own home," Onno responded. He fixed his somber blue eyes on her.

"Have you told her yet to stop calling you?

"No, I haven't, but I tried telling David the phone calls were too disruptive."

"And what did he say?"

"That I should be more understanding because she is lonely."

"She's his mother, but he is putting the responsibility on you."

"He tries to humour her, but I end up talking to her much more than he does."

"He is passive aggressive and you are a martyr."

"I'm trying to be civilized, Onno," Sara said, unable to mask her irritation. "You'd like me to scream at her, wouldn't you?"

"It's not me who wants to scream," Onno, said, "it's you. Think about it. This session will give you a lot to think about." He handed her the 90 minute cassette on which he had recorded the session. "Listen to it and then you'll have a better idea what you have to do. You can rest in the front room as long as you wish, if you feel you're not ready to go out into the street yet."

"I think I'll do that." As she rose from the armchair, Sara felt dizzy and hypersensitive. The noise of traffic on Ste. Catherine street would be unbearable now. Attempting to cross the street might be fatal. She was drenched with sweat from the session. First, she would change into her spare set of clothes in Onno's bathroom, then she would lie on the sofa until she felt confident enough to return to the babel of Montreal.

Yeshim Ternar